PROJECT NOVA

Somewhere, in a top-secret site, a mysterious government project is about to be launched. It will bring forth a revolutionary form of energy so powerful, it can transform the world.

IMPOSSIBLE MISSION

Sterling Mann, scientifically bred super-spy, genius of modern technology, has stumbled on the plans for Nova and found its fatal flaw . . . the flaw that will trigger nuclear meltdown and plunge the world into a Black Hole. From Morocco to the Himalayas to treacherous ice caves below the Antarctic floor, Mann is caught in a harrowing race against time. He must find Nova and stop the lethal count-down . . . before Nova destroys the world!

FIRE
BELOW
ZERO

Nico Mastorakis
and
Barnaby Conrad

A DELL BOOK

Published by
Dell Publishing Co., Inc.
1 Dag Hammarskjold Plaza
New York, New York 10017

Dell ® TM 681510, Dell Publishing Co., Inc.

ISBN: 0-440-12524-3

Printed in the United States of America
First printing—June 1981

CHAPTER ONE

October 9, 1982

As the attractive, thirty-four-year-old brunette came out of the telephone booth into the night, she saw death waiting for her. She did not actually see *them* . . . only the car, the long, black Cadillac, which had an unmistakable lethal look, a visible aura of evil about its sleek exterior, and she knew that *they* were inside.

They were across the intersection and down half a block in the glistening wet gloom of late night in Manhattan, and there wasn't another vehicle in sight. She sensed that this was it and she was scared. But how had they found out that *she knew* so soon?

Her first instinct was to go back into the phone booth and call for help. But whom? She had just telephoned Sterling to tell him of her astounding discovery, the news event of the century, but there had been only the answering machine. She had tried to reach him earlier as she worked on the rough draft at her office . . . it would be useless to call the office, for she had been the last one out.

Police, yes, but could she impress them with what still might be only a nervous hunch? Then she saw the black car slide slowly forward. The phone booth could be riddled by bullets right through the glass before she finished dialing. No use presenting them with such a well-illuminated target . . . she would have to play it cool.

Walk, don't run, baby, and hope to God someone comes along!

She started down the street walking briskly in her high heels; a good-looking woman out for an evening stroll, perhaps they'd think she was just a hooker and cruise on by. But then she heard the insinuating purr of the Cadillac's motor and she could no longer control her feet. She found herself kicking off her shoes and running. Running flat out. She had been athletic at Bryn Mawr not so many years ago and had stayed in good shape.

"Dear God," she prayed as she sprinted for the corner, "let someone be there!"

There was a taxi, but it was headed away from her.

"Help!" she screamed after it, but the cab kept going.

"Help me!"

Her voice seemed to echo futilely, reverberating through the wasteland of darkened office buildings, and hope of rescue waned rapidly as she kept pounding the concrete relentlessly with her now sore feet.

She looked back as she ran and saw the Cadillac with its faceless crew loom around the corner, lights off. By the time she panted to the end of the block, the car was less than fifty yards from her and gaining fast.

As she rounded the corner at Fifty-fourth she saw it . . . saw her salvation: the crowd in front of Equinox, the old Studio 54.

She put on a final burst of speed as she heard the car screech to a stop just behind her. Glancing back over her shoulder, she saw the three men jump out of the Cadillac. And then, suddenly, she was on the fringe of the crowd and pushing in among them, hoping to be swallowed up by the mass of people.

"Hey, lady!" someone whined. "We're waitin' to get in too, y'know!"

"Bitch!" snarled another.

She could see the men not far behind her.

"Please, oh, God, please let me in," she cried out.

There was something in her terror-filled face that caused them to part and to let her go through, right up to within sight of the security guards.

"Alexandra Robinson!" She called out her name. "You know me, you *know* me!"

One of the guards spotted her, raised a finger, and a moment later she was inside the entrance. Right behind her the three men pushed forward and were confronted by the guards.

"Hold it, fellas," said one of the guards laconically.

"We gotta get in!"

The guard looked him over. "I don't think you gotta get in." He turned to his partner. "Jim, you think they gotta get in?"

"But we're with her . . . Miss Robinson."

"Funny, said she was alone."

"But we have to . . ."

"Get lost, fellas. No hard feelings but no dice tonight. And next time, try lookin' a little less straight—might help your chances."

The men hesitated, glanced at each other, and went back to the car. A short time later a tall skeletal man costumed as Mae West with two "plumber's friends" on his chest was readily admitted, even though he was not known to the guards. After him there appeared a rotund, almost spherical man dressed as a lion tamer, holding a small mirrored cage and sporting a multicolored whip under his arm.

"M'lords," said the fat man in a strong Yorkshire accent, "Morley Flaversham at your orders!"

With a grandiose sweep he doffed his high silk hat, making an elaborate bow as he did.

The two security doormen looked at each other, shrugged, and in a moment the bizarre man was inside the disco. He was almost submerged in its Felliniesque surrealism. Except for the title and, supposedly, the owners, nothing had changed inside Studio 54.

The Englishman looked around himself appreciatively, a little smile on his fat, moist lips. As the computerized neon lights counterpointed the primal jungle blast of the music, he looked in wonder at the frenzied dancing. He seemed almost an amiable, bewildered grandpa, watching the young disport themselves. The fat man studied the decor, the half-moon snorting cocaine from a neon spoon as it traveled across the spacious room, the swiveling mirrors that were lowered down from the ceiling almost to the tops of the heads of the gyrating dancers. The man's nostrils flared like those of a carousel horse, then contracted as he savored the stench, the fresh sweat blended with carnations and ambergris and Shalimar and Speedstik and Jack Daniel's and margarita mix and incense and, of course, the sticky-sweet smell of cannabis pervading every corner.

The fat man waddled past Bill, the bartender, and barely glanced at Alexandra as he headed for the upper part of the discotheque. He ascended the burgundy velvet stairs, passed the mezzanine, and ambled onto the great balcony. In the gloom were scattered human relics, bizarrely and scantily clad. One tired dancer was smoking pot, two others were off together sniffing some white powder, and one rather muscular body of indeterminate sex had its bobbing head in the lap of a person dressed as Abraham Lincoln. Detached, the Englishman took a seat as far as possible from the others, but where he could still command a view of the dancers. From an inside pocket he took out a pair of small, powerful binoculars.

Now he watched as Alexandra canvassed the room, searching for the three thugs. Not seeing them, she went into the ladies' room to remove her ragged hosiery and inspect and bathe her feet with wet paper towels. He was beginning to wonder if she might have slipped out a back way when she finally emerged and went to the bar.

As he watched her through the binoculars, he could see her chatting with the bartender in a friendly way. He noticed that she fingered the locket with the expensive medallion that he had sent with that precious little card, "From your devoted fan!" He'd been quite sure she wouldn't be able to resist it, expecially with the price of gold so antic. He peered through his binoculars at the distinguished-looking older man who had stopped to speak to Alexandra. They seemed to be talking animatedly, and although he could read lips, the angle made it too difficult to determine precisely what was being said. But from the facial expressions he knew it was merely the usual courtesies.

Alexandra was nervously looking around the room. Thank God, for the moment she was safe.

Tomorrow the police. And, of course, Sterling. She sipped her drink and watched the dancers in her relief. Now a lithe panther of a man emerged and she knew him as Satin Joe. Joe Nickle, "Satin Joe," was in his element and in great form. Acorn bald, he was dressed in a white and silver sequined bolero. There was no shirt under his vest, and his smooth cinnamon skin, glistening with perspiration, was displayed to advantage. He clasped his fingers around her wrist and pulled her to the dance floor. Alexandra shouted a protest because of her damaged feet, but it was drowned under a wave of two megawatts of blaring music and then she found herself glad to be in Satin Joe's arms.

Better this way, she thought. Now, in the brilliantly lit circle of dancers, she felt more secure. Who could kill her in front of so many witnesses . . . and how? A small smile of relief parted her lips, and she began to move with the beat. Strangely, her feet did not hurt. Perhaps they were numb.

They danced and they danced . . . Lord, how they danced! The beat, the constant tom-tom of the melody, Latin now, the wail, the screech, the threnody, the bleat, the lament of the music grabbed them, held them, controlled them like marionettes. Touching or not touching, they moved together as one, more together than most couples in bed in the act of copulating. Up and down, in and out, they undulated, they swayed, they shivered, they clutched, they grabbed, they pushed each other, they convulsed, they jerked, they struck each other, they slapped themselves, their bodies did everything their owners told them to do and more, and all of it synchronized with the relentless beat of the deafening music.

Upstairs the smiling fat man watched them as though mesmerized, a lovable old voyeur. He sighed as though reluctant to end such a diverting spectacle; his gloved hand opened the mirrored door of the small cage. Carefully, he extracted its occupant. The creature's big eyes glowed over the rubber cap that covered its mouth like a surgeon's mask.

"Ah, my little *fledermaus*, my little *murciélago*, my *abrenoite* . . ."

The Englishman stroked his pet gently, almost tenderly, as his fingertips clamped its wings to its sides. Then he carefully removed the cap, holding the creature up, away from his fat stomach. He could tell by its darting eyes that it had already detected the subsonic signals. Smoothly, the fat man raised his hand and launched the weapon into the dim, smoke-filled air.

In a few rapid wing movements, the vampire bat was over the dancers, desperately trying to pinpoint the alluring electronic signals from below. Back and forth it zigzagged, its feral face avidly searching. Then suddenly it folded its wings, dipped, and diving like a dagger, it plunged down toward the couple in the center, straight down at the woman's head. The bat barely paused at its target, just the microsecond it took to bite the scalp, and then it careened off into the darkness of the balcony. No one saw it, least of all Satin Joe, who now grabbed Alexandra to him. He spun her body into him and around him, like a matador with a cape executing the Mariposa pass. People applauded as the dancing couple revolved and then came to a slow, graceful stop at the same time that the music ended. Satin Joe started to bow, but he felt the woman sag into his arms.

"Hey, baby," he whispered, "straighten up and get your act together!"

But her eyes were half closed, lids fluttering, and her body was a dead weight against him.

"Too much, huh, baby?"

Satin Joe put his right arm around her body, draped her left arm around his shoulder, and half dragged, half carried her over to a couch. He sat down beside her and slapped her gray face once. Her breathing was shallow and irregular; the curare had done its work.

"Alexandra! Hear me?"

She didn't answer.

"Well," he stood up. "Sweet dreams, baby."

The man sighed, suddenly unsure and shaken. But she wasn't the first person to pass out here.

He went to the bar and quickly forgot about Alexandra.

"Massa, give me a margarita," he said to the bartender. "Puhleez."

"On the house," growled the man.

"You are too kind, señor," said Satin Joe. "Wow, whatta night!"

"What happened to Alexandra?" mused the bar-man.

"Oh, yeah," Satin Joe said, frowning. "Alex! Better see how that nice lady is doin'."

He downed his drink, slid off the stool, and started back toward the couch where Alexandra Robinson's corpse lay.

In the dark of the balcony, the Englishman shoved a mint in his mouth.

The bat appeared out of the dark, flew low over the unsuspecting patrons, and landed smoothly on the Englishman's gloved hand. He replaced the cap on its snout, gave it a placating stroke, and put it back in its cage.

A moment later the fat man, the mirrored cage, and the bat had been swallowed up by the dark-ness of the velvet-padded door marked EXIT.

CHAPTER TWO

April 12, 1945

On this day four men and four women, each under the age of thirty-three and over the age of twenty and each unique in his or her own way, entered the small auditorium at the Dease Lake Laboratory in Colorado to be briefed regarding their part in one of the most incredible experiments in eugenics ever conducted.

As they filed into the empty room, escorted by two plainclothes security guards, the eight selectees gave off an aura of vitality and excitement. After sitting down at random, they nodded shyly at one another, having never met before but knowing that they were now part of a most important oneness.

Almost immediately the door opened at the far

end of the room and an imposing bearded man appeared. An unlit pipe jutted from his mouth, and carrying a briefcase, he strode to the podium.

"Good morning," he said warmly, "everyone." He had a slight speech impediment, not quite a stammer but a tiny hesitation before certain words that had the effect of making those words seem more important. Otherwise his voice was strong and carried enormous authority. One could see his tobacco-stained teeth as he smiled mock-apologetically at the cliché he intoned: "I suppose you're wondering why I have called you all here together . . ."

Most of the eight responded with smiles, and some with nervous laughter.

"I am Doctor Henry Monroe," said the man, moving casually from behind the podium and dropping his plump body into the captain's chair beside it. He put his pipe into his breast pocket. "In the next few months I hope we will all become friends. I know we shall." Then, with a little intake of breath, he added, "We will have to."

He was short, and although only thirty-six years old, his black beard had two white streaks, one on either side of his chin, and his curly hair was slate colored.

"I trust you are all happy with your accommodations?"

The octet nodded as one, affirmatively and with smiles of appreciation.

"I'm sorry that the beautiful scenery has had to

be parceled off—some of you have suites with
views of the mountains and others with views of
the lake—but we shall trade around in a few weeks
so as to be fair. If you have any complaints, any
. . . wants for your comfort, anything at all from
Alka Seltzer to caviar"—he turned in his chair—
"just tell Horace here about it."

A tiny black man, smaller than a jockey and
dressed in a white suit, had entered at the door
behind Dr. Monroe. Of an indeterminate age, the
black gnome stood there with a large grin on his
pinched face.

Horace broadened his grin, gave a deep bow,
stepped back, and the door closed.

"Horace and everyone else here, some fifty-six
of us in all, want your stay at Dease Lake Laboratory to be, not only important, but also one of the
pleasantest times of your lives."

He took off his rimless glasses and cleaned
them with his handkerchief.

"Now, before we get down to 'brohss tocks,' as
my old anatomy professor at Harvard used to say,
allow me to introduce you to one another. As you
know, each of you has been chosen from . . . a
different part of the country, selected from some
twenty-six thousand Americans who were
screened by me and my staff. Each of you has
qualified because of special abilities or talents or
traits or physical conditions. And of course, ultimately, because of your hearty and courageous
willingness to . . . participate in this . . . this

. . ." his stammer became more pronounced, "this experiment that we have called 'Project Alpha.'

" 'Innovative' and 'bizarre' and 'revolutionary' and . . . 'visionary' . . . are words all too . . . tame for it, so let's just say that you are all pioneers and unique and that what we are all doing here will be of . . . immense . . . value . . . to the United States."

He paused thoughtfully for a long interval, then he said almost casually, "I might add that Franklin Roosevelt authorized this project back in 1939. I talked to him in Georgia yesterday and he knows of our meeting today, and in spite of his enormous preoccupation with wartime problems, he knows about each and every one of you. He knows, in fact, as much as I and my staff do. You and our . . . project have been a very special thing to him for . . . four years."

The listeners reacted to this statement in various ways; one woman suddenly let out a little moan and began dabbing at her eyes.

Dr. Monroe looked at her curiously. Then he said, "So much for flag waving . . . upward and onward . . ."

He opened his briefcase and took out some papers.

"Will you kindly stand when I call your name, and as briefly as possible, I will explain who you are and why you've been chosen.

"Let us start with the oldest of you, for no particular reason, except . . ." he smiled, "except that I have read all three of his monumental books and hope he will autograph them for me later. I give you . . ." Dr. Monroe gestured at a tall, skeletal, round-shouldered man in the back row. "I give you Robinson Eugene Bergh."

All in the group turned with astonishment and admiration to the man, who ducked his head, shyly pushed the lock of blond hair back from his pale forehead, and barely rose from his seat in acknowledgment.

"I see that you also know the books of the renowned philosopher and free thinker and astonishing brain that is Doctor Bergh. I hope in the ensuing few months that he will find time to try to explain his writings to a poor layman like myself."

Dr. Monroe riffled through his notes although it was clear he did not need them. "Next, the youngest . . . Nancy Vreeland." A dumpy, persimmon-cheeked young woman bounced out of her front-row seat, turned, and smiled at the rest of the group.

"Nancy may not have the IQ of Doctor Bergh, but she is nonetheless vital to the . . . success of our project. Nancy's reason for being here is a physical one . . . she has been proven to be . . . immune to almost every disease known to man . . . or woman. Nancy, I want you to thank your parents for encouraging you to participate here."

She nodded, obviously pleased, then sat down.

"*Ahora,*" Dr. Monroe said. "*Les voy a presenter a una dama de mucho genio y talento . . . Señorita Granger!*"

He gestured toward a Nordic-looking woman in her mid-twenties, thin lipped, straw hair pulled back in a bun, and with glasses as thick as the bottom of a bottle.

"How did I do, Ilsa?" Dr. Monroe asked like a little boy.

"*Bastante bien,*" replied the woman solemnly. "There was just one thing . . . were you speaking Italian or French?"

Dr. Monroe sighed as the group laughed. "Linguistics were never my strong suit. But they . . . certainly are Doctor Ilsa Granger's. She comes to us from Princeton, where she is a full professor, and at her tender age . . . she is quite possibly the country's top expert in linguistics. She not only speaks twenty-two languages, she reads another dozen. I didn't even know there *were* that many languages! You will understand her importance to Project Alpha soon, but meanwhile, Ilsa, *bienvenida de todo mi corazón.*"

The woman smiled and sat down.

Dr. Monroe glanced at his notes.

"I now introduce you to a gentleman who is an expert in a field that I know a little better than languages . . . Stephen Balfour Alfreds, who occupies the Radowitz Chair at Yale for physics. I don't believe there's a more . . . exalted position in the field. He is also an inventor with thirty-three patents to his credit. One of his inventions, about which I'll tell you later, is something that many of us use every day."

Although thirty-one years old Dr. Alfreds looked young enough to be a college student. He grinned and clenched his hands together over his head as he stood up.

"Good luck," he said. "Good luck!"

"Doctor Alfreds, I'm sure, will be able to convince us all that light does not always travel faster than sound by cocktail time. And speaking of that, there *will* be a cocktail hour in the main lounge every day for those of you who care, and let me hastily add that I care very much. But for those who don't, do what you want; play tennis, go riding or fishing or hiking or attend the movies in this little theater. Tonight, I believe, is *Casablanca*. Do whatever strikes your fancy. We want to . . . we *must* . . . create an atmosphere of, you know, what shall I say? . . . *Gemütlichkeit?* Is that correct, Ilsa?"

"*Gemütlichkeit,*" echoed Ilsa Granger, nodding, although the word sounded quite different the way she said it.

"Tom, do you speak a lot of languages?" asked Dr. Monroe addressing a stubby, totally bald man in the second row. He did not even have eyebrows. The man stood up slowly.

"Doctor, I once had a hell of a feel for pig Latin, but it's a little rusty these days."

"Be that as it may, Thomas Clarence Washington, but we sent out a secret ballot to dozens of faculty heads asking them to nominate their idea of the top young psychologists of the country who also had the highest moral qualities, and unanimously they picked you."

The man shrugged, grinned, and said as he sat down, "Can't lose 'em all, and perhaps the fact that I bribed all those who voted with an unlimited supply of genuine English gin had a little something to do with it."

"I am convinced of that," said Dr. Monroe solemnly.

"Next we come to a man who has given all of us so much pleasure. How many of you saw the play *Holiday in the Heather*?"

Several people raised their hands and one said, "I saw the movie."

"Gawd, wasn't it positively excremental!" exclaimed a voice. It came from the young man of riveting handsomeness in the front row. With his thick black eyebrows and obsidian hair, he looked like Tyrone Power.

"The play was about a dowdy little Scottish schoolmarm," he said, "so naturally, who else should bring it to glorious full color on the screen but that dowdy little Scots girl, Ingrid Bergman? In all fairness, it was not her fault."

"Ladies and gentlemen, you have now met Ernest Thompson Fitzpatrick, who, at twenty-seven, is the only American to have two hits on Broadway simultaneously. I believe his qualifications for this project are obvious!

"Less obvious, perhaps . . ." He beckoned to a twenty-eight-year-old woman to rise. She had a protruding lower lip and a distressed expression, and constantly twirled a lock of her long black hair. Her watery eyes were of such a pale, milky blue that it was hard to distinguish where her irises left off and the white began. She did not bother to rise.

"Laura Rosen. I wish I could explain Laura to you. Perhaps she could not even do it herself. You see, Laura is not so special at first glance, although she is one of triplets. She is married to a fine fellow, owner of a hardware store in Fresno, who has so gallantly agreed to let her come here. And why is she here? She is one of the most . . . gifted people in the field of ESP that Doctor Rhine and his staff at Duke University have ever encountered. Positively astounding scores on those tests . . . you know . . . when she's in one room and names the cards as they are turned in another room.

"Last but not least, we come to Gale . . . Gale O'Brien. Gale, would you mind standing for our pleasure?"

The girl smiled good-naturedly and stood up. While her blond hair and wholesome face could have graced the cover of any magazine, it was her six-foot body that was so staggeringly beautiful.

Firm breasts strained under her silk blouse, below them a narrow waist and superbly long legs.

"I don't think you'll find it surprising that Gale was Miss California two years ago. But I should also tell you that she was graduated from UCLA with honors, majoring in painting and sculpture, and that she is a classical pianist of some . . ."

At that moment the door behind Dr. Monroe was jerked open and Horace lurched in. His face was contorted and wet with tears.

"Doctor Monroe!" He struggled to get the words out. "He's dead! He's dead!"

"Who's dead?" exclaimed a startled Dr. Monroe.

"Oh, Lord, I jus' now heard it on the radio . . . President Roosevelt jus' now died!"

Laura Rosen nodded silently as she dabbed at her eyes.

It was a subdued group that met with Dr. Monroe in the auditorium the next morning. Dr. Monroe gave a brief but eloquent and emotional tribute to "my friend, my hero, FDR." Then he added firmly, "But his passing will not alter our project one whit, and the most sincere expression of our love and loyalty would be to get on with it as soon as possible."

It was then announced that Laura Rosen had submitted her request to withdraw from the program and that her place would be filled by one Laney Barnes, an attractive young widow. It was not surprising to those who had noticed Laura's excessive grief over the death of the President, although the official excuse was her husband's change of heart.

"And just what is this project really all about?" questioned Dr. Bergh from his seat in the back of the auditorium. "We have a right to know."

"Ah, I was afraid someone would ask that!" said Dr. Monroe, taking the unlit pipe out of his mouth.

The rest of the group laughed.

"Yes, you do have a right to know. Seriously," continued Monroe, "I cannot be too specific at this point. I will tell you that it has to do with a never-before-tried experiment in eugenics and that it is considered to be of great importance by many people, including our late President. Would you be generous enough to accept those generalities as an explanation for the time being? Could I belabor the point by saying that it could be of enormous importance to our country?"

They all nodded thoughtfully.

"Good! Now, I shall give you a little background in controlled genetics . . ."

In a clear informal talk Dr. Monroe explained how, in 1896, John Humphrey Noyes, the founder of the Oneida Colony in New York State and a Utopian Socialist, decided to put Galton's theory into practice, since: "Every racehorse, every straight-backed bull, every premium pig tells us what we can do and what we must do for man."

In what was considered to be the first organized nucleus of a eugenics society, Noyes had conducted an experiment to breed healthy perfect specimens by "matching those most advanced in health and perfection." The women pledged that they would become "martyrs to science," and with that the first American experiments in eugenics began.

Some forty years later eugenics became a not so openly admitted, but still deeply rooted obsession of America's twenty-sixth president. Theodore Roosevelt, the Bull Moose himself, once pounded his desk and asserted: "The emphasis should be laid on getting desirable people to breed!"

Dr. Monroe added, "This quote could just as well have come from the lips of countless political functionaries in Nazi Germany in the last ten years, couldn't it?"

The young Nancy Vreeland jumped up. "Doctor, are you saying we're going to be in some Nazi experiment?"

The others smiled and Nancy, embarrassed, sat down.

"No, dear, nothing like that. Though, I must tell you, we have studied several of the German ideas for creating a master race, and of course, selective breeding is at the heart of our project and you knew *that* much when you agreed to come here. We have picked the finest examples of Americans in different and varied ways, and we intend to study their cross progeny."

He then went on to explain, with the utmost delicacy, how this would be done: In the next few months there would be a social and athletic program, a "getting-to-know-you time." At the end of that period, well, purely and simply, they would pair off, and hopefully the four women would become pregnant.

"At that time, when we are sure all four women are pregnant, we will be totally specific about the reasons for this experiment. If anyone wishes to back out of the project, please do so now. No one will hold it against you, we have plenty of substitutes willing to fill your places, and you will be paid in full, just as though you had gone ahead with us."

He looked out over his audience.

"Anyone else for dropping out?"

No one answered.

"Good!" said Dr. Monroe, smiling. "I knew we had a fine group. However, if at any time at all, anyone wishes to drop out, feel free to do so." He looked down paternally at Nancy Vreeland. "This is no Nazi concentration camp, Nancy."

The girl blushed and and smiled.

"Now I want you all to meet someone who will be increasingly important to you—Irene Schmidt."

He turned and through the door came a handsome woman in a nurse's uniform. She was thirty-five and would have been very pretty if her face had not worn a worried look.

"Doctor Schmidt is invaluable to me in many ways. Only she knows as much about this endeavor as I do. I could give you a long list of her credits and accomplishments . . . but let us just say that no one in the world knows more about eugenics than she does."

The woman smiled, not egotistically, but simply accepting a known fact; she was, after all, primarily a dealer in facts. She studied the audience, almost sympathetically, her pale blue eyes virtually all pupils devoid of irises. She held two fingers to her temples continually, as though she had a bad headache.

"Should anything happen to me, Doctor Schmidt would take over. Would you care to say anything, Doctor?"

The woman cleared her throat and looked nervous.

"Nothing, really, except welcome, and you are all to be commended. It will not be easy."

Her voice trailed off.

"What she means is," Dr. Monroe hastily interjected, "the training will be rigorous, but the rewards will be worth it, right?"

Dr. Schmidt barely nodded.

"Now I see it is exercise time," said Dr. Monroe glancing at his watch. "Let us proceed to the gymnasium."

The eight people rose and filed out of the auditorium, chatting among themselves pleasantly; the night before with its gourmet dinner, champagne, movie, and piano concert by Gale O'Brien had loosened them all up considerably.

Dr. Monroe started to gather up his notes as Irene Schmidt walked over to him.

"Why didn't you tell them?" she said. "Henry, why?"

"Tell them?" repeated Dr. Monroe, vaguely, barely hesitating as he put his papers into his briefcase.

"Tell them the truth!" said Dr. Schmidt.

"Irene," sighed Dr. Monroe. "We've had this all out, we agreed!"

"You've got to tell them," she insisted.

"Look, Irene," said Monroe sternly, taking the pipe from his mouth. "Do you want this project to succeed or fail?"

"How dare you ask me that! Who was the one who taught you everything you know about MPO?"

"Oh, come on now, Irene! We both learned about multiple-parent-offspring from Kleeman."

"Yes, but who did it first? Who did it with real living creatures?"

"You, you, you!" Dr. Monroe said exasperatedly. "You got lucky with mice—that's true—but who raised it up to the rhesus? And what's that go to do with—"

"Henry, these aren't mice or monkeys or dogs—they are people, don't you understand? Fine, if they know what they are getting into—but they *must* know!"

"They know they're going to—like mice—they're going to be bred. They know that! They knew that before they even came here! So?"

"So they don't know the rest!"

"Irene, if they knew the rest, they'd know what you and I and the President of the United States knows and no one else in this whole fucking world knows!"

His use of the crude word, so unlike him, was a slap across her face.

"Henry, tell them, it's only fair!"

"Fair!" he exploded. "Irene, are you a scientist—or a woman?"

She gasped. "That is the rudest thing I've heard today!"

"All right," he said apologetically. "Are you a scientist first and foremost?"

"I won't dignify that with an answer. If you don't know that after eight years, then—to use your term—go fuck yourself!"

He grinned slowly and put his arm around her.

"You and your anatomical impossibilities!"

She melted slightly. "*Improbabilities*," she corrected. "There was a man in Ceylon in 1856 who . . ."

"Hey," he said, "knock it off—let's go get some coffee."

"Henry—tell them—those poor women."

He sighed. "What about the men?"

"Are you kidding? It's the women who are going to lose!"

"I remember a wonderful song I heard when I was an exchange student in Madrid . . . '*Lo mismo pierde un hombre como una mujer.*'"

"Meaning?"

"A man—he loses just a much as a woman."

"Henry, to that, and I say it kindly, I say, bullshit! Especially in this case! What have the men got to lose? A one-night stand, big deal!"

Dr. Monroe's tone suddenly grew angry. "Look Irene, darling, Doctor Schmidt, nobody held a gun to these ladies' lovely heads."

"Maybe not a gun! But what about the carrot? Fifteen thousand dollars is not to be sneezed at, for four months, quote, work, unquote."

"Agreed! But they know what they are doing and—"

"But that's just the point, you boob, they don't know what they are doing!"

He grabbed her upper arm fiercely in a bruising grip. "Do not call me names, madam! And do not forget that you are privy to the secret of one of the great undertakings of our time!"

"Let go of me!" she commanded calmly. "Go have your coffee—I will have mine in the laboratory. And when we meet at lunch, let us try to behave civilly."

Laura Rosen was not missed. Within a week it was clear that the handsome playwright, Fitzpatrick, and Laney Barnes were a pair, experiment or no experiment. They made no bones about their feelings for each other, and it was general knowledge that they were sleeping in the same room. Dr. Monroe had to advise them to kindly take precautions; she should not conceive before the others if the experiment was to be a success.

As for other pairings, Dr. Monroe and Irene Schmidt had worried about how it was to be done. By lot seemed logical but somehow not right; as Irene pointed out repeatedly to Dr. Monroe, these were humans, not mice. It had been suggested, of course, that artificial insemination be used, but Doctor Monroe kept saying, "In this experiment, the psyche is all important."

As it turned out, they needn't have worried; nature took care of it. Couples found themselves gradually, if unexpectedly. Shy and brilliant Dr. Bergh, for example, was immediately taken with the young, uneducated Nancy Vreeland. Gale O'Brien, the former Miss California, who Dr. Monroe had initially thought would align herself with the handsome playwright, chose instead the ugliest man of the group, the totally hairless, short psychologist, Thomas Clarence Washington. Finally, when Dr. Monroe saw Ilsa Granger, the linguist, and Stephen Alfreds, the mathematician-physicist, going for a row on the lake, he knew he had been relieved of the rather embarrassing task of assigning mates.

There were no further complications. One month later, sooner than they had thought necessary, Dr. Monroe and Irene let the eight people know that it was time for the experiment to begin. The couples made jokes among themselves, now calling the project "Operation Copulation."

Six weeks later all four women were proven to be pregnant, having conceived under the finest of conditions—all four mentally and physically ripe for conception. There was a feeling of excitement and jubilation among them. The fathers stayed on, a requirement of the project, yet all would have done so anyway.

When Laney and Fitzpatrick were married in the auditorium, the party afterward was a joyous one. Dr. Monroe was best man, Irene Schmidt matron of honor, Gale played the piano, and Horace, little Horace, sang "Oh Promise Me" in a mellow baritone. Dr. Monroe offered unlimited bottles of Moët & Chandon but few people drank—they were on another kind of high, the exhilaration of being involved in an exciting project together . . . sharing an important secret.

Then two months later came the blow.

A very solemn Dr. Monroe called the eight people into the auditorium. Dr. Irene Schmidt was conspicuous by her absence.

"I have sad news for you," he said, puffing on his unlit pipe. "Due to factors entirely beyond our control, this experiment must be . . . aborted . . . and I use the word advisedly."

A murmur ran through the group.

"What do you mean?" demanded Nancy Vreeland.

"I mean, dear Nancy, the experiment was a failure . . . I am terribly sorry . . . and you must submit to surgery to terminate your pregnancy."

"You mean—an abortion?" said Dr. Bergh.

"Oh, no!" Nancy cried.

"I will not!" said Laney Barnes Fitzpatrick hotly. "We are *married*, you know!"

"I will not either," said Gale O'Brien. "Will we, Tom?"

Dr. Monroe sighed wearily. "First of all, according to your contracts, it is spelled out that you must submit to an abortion at any time during the experiment. You all read it, you signed it, presumably you understood it. Secondly, and I know this sounds terribly crass—we can never really compensate for your loss with money—but the contract also states that should you be required to abort, you will be paid double the amount, which I believe would be thirty thousand dollars."

He took the pipe from his mouth and cleared his throat.

"Thirdly, I think you will want to have the abortions. You've perhaps wondered about those daily injections both the men and the women have been taking. I'm not permitted to tell why we gave them to you, but we thought the serum would prove a great value to the unborn children. Our mistake—my mistake—was monumental! We have learned through the laboratory tests that the effect of the serum was quite the opposite—every one of the four children you women are carrying would prove to be mongoloid if brought to term . . . Down's syndrome."

The women gasped.

"I am truly sorry," Doctor Monroe said with tears in his eyes. "You men—my friends—are free to leave immediately. You women, who I've grown to love, your abortions will be scheduled in the morning. You should stay on a few days more. I would . . . like to . . . say . . . that . . ."

He struggled with his stammer, then overcome by emotion, he lurched from the podium and out of the door behind him.

Irene Schmidt was standing there with her arms folded as Monroe came out wiping his eyes with his handkerchief.

"Oh, Hank," she said, "what an act."

Dr. Monroe put the handkerchief into his pocket.

"Not acting," he said hoarsely.

She shrugged and said, "Well, I guess I'd better get the operating rooms set up."

"Has Lena arrived?" asked Dr. Monroe.

"Naturally," replied Irene Schmidt. "Do I ever fail you?"

"No," conceded Dr. Monroe with a deep sigh. "No, you do not."

CHAPTER THREE

Four surgical units in four operating rooms were set up for the historical experiment. Four gurneys were wheeled in, the patients draped, legs placed in stirrups and the anesthesia countdown begun; Dr. Monroe wanted the women delivered as simultaneously as possible. Soon four embryos, immersed in warm normal saline solution, were rushed to the laboratory where Dr. Monroe was prepared for their reception.

Rapidly, but with control and gentleness, he transferred each embryo from the saline solution to a beaker set in a water bath at normal body temperature. Into this he carefully measured a chemical substance from a small flask, and as he anxiously watched, he could perceive the disintegration of the connective tissues and could only pray that the life force within the individual cellular structures remained intact.

In the next step of the process the embryonic fluid was filtered and rinsed with warm saline, and the combined cells were treated with a substance of a gellike consistency. Consolidated into one large beaker, they were then placed in an incubator.

The following ten hours were as difficult for both Monroe and Dr. Schmidt as any period on a conventional obstetrical ward might be. Through the window of the incubator, they could observe the contents of the beaker. They drank coffee, paced back and forth, peered into the incubator, then drank more coffee, repeating the routine endlessly, saying very little but exchanging frequent wan smiles.

At last they were confident that they were seeing a definite clumping effect as the cells began to join forces to produce what Dr. Monroe called his "communal zygote." The jubilation was tempered by their profound weariness and the knowledge that there was still one more all-important step ahead of them.

On the operating table lay a large peasant woman of German extraction who had been flown in from Montana. Her name was Lena Knarek. Monroe took the fetal organism and implanted it within the uterine chamber of the surrogate mother.

As he stripped off his gloves, he closed his eyes

and tipped back his head for a moment. When he again opened his eyes, he found Irene watching him intently. With a small wry smile he held up his hand for her to see. His fingers were crossed . . . scientifically.

That was all there was to it—yet it had taken four solid years of experimentation with hundreds of mice, monkeys, and a dozen dogs to achieve this result.

And what *would* the result be? Would the embryo take hold? Could this abnormal conception result in a normal birth?

Irene Schmidt put aside her resentments in the ensuing months as they waited restlessly for the results of their bizarre experiment.

Lena, thirty-eight, was a healthy and cheerful uneducated woman, not particularly interested in the experiment. Divorced, she had eight other children back in Billings. She needed money and was not going to form any sentimental attachments to the unborn child, which was why she had been chosen.

From the prenatal tests Dr. Monroe was convinced from the beginning that it was to be a healthy child. When a male baby was delivered easily and quickly on September 19, 1946, Dr. Monroe and Dr. Schmidt attended the momentous debut—and were ecstatic.

The crying child that Dr. Monroe held up was beyond their wildest hopes: He was dark-haired, large boned, weighing in at eleven pounds. He had only one distinguishing feature—one eye was brown, the other blue.

"No," said Dr. Monroe. "He is handsome." And with a little catch in his voice, "The handsomest child I've ever delivered."

"What shall we name him?" she asked, taking the baby.

"What else?" asked Dr. Monroe. "Sterling, of course, the acronym of his eight parents' first names."

"But is that going to be his first name or his last?" she asked as she cleaned the child.

"I think—his first. What about a last?"

"Something terribly simple—it should be simple, don't you think? He is a man—the first man, the first poly-parented man. Shall we call him Sterling Mann? Or Adam Sterling?"

"Whatever you decide, Irene."

Then uncharacteristically Henry Monroe suddenly kissed her on the mouth in front of everyone in the delivery room.

"Thank you—thank you," he murmured.

Dr. Schmidt actually blushed. "For what?"

"For being such a good scientist and such a good woman."

Dr. Schmidt busied herself with the baby.

"I am just sorry for those poor other women—they'll never know what a gorgeous child they produced."

"Someday, perhaps," replied Dr. Monroe. "Yes, maybe someday they will know . . . perhaps the world will know. Meanwhile, everyone in this room is sworn to secrecy about . . . about this procedure, about this event, this milestone. And, as of tomorrow, we will start to phase out this place. Tomorrow I will be telling the staff that they can return to their regular work, but of course I shall have to remind them that discussing any phase of what went on here will immediately forfeit the otherwise guaranteed bonus and retirement benefits. As soon as we finish here, I want the entire staff alerted to meet in the lounge, where I shall stand you all to some champagne prior to the celebration banquet I so optimistically ordered. You have no idea how grateful I am that it is not to be a consolation offering!"

The nurses smiled and nodded and one of them took the baby from Dr. Schmidt and went through the glass door to the little nursery. Irene Schmidt watched it go with eyes filled with tears of happiness and affection.

As they left the delivery room, Dr. Schmidt held two fingers to her temples as though to push away some pressure.

"Henry, promise me that no one takes care of that boy except me." She closed her eyes. "Please!"

"Promised!" he assured her. "Migraine bad?"

"Just stress . . . it's been a long day . . . a long period of uncertainty . . . a . . . wrestling with morality and ethics . . ." She shot him a quick smile. "You know what I mean."

A month later the headaches were discovered to be due to a brain tumor.

"I've got to tell you something," she whispered on her deathbed.

"Sleep, darling," said Dr. Monroe in a distraught guttural.

"Wasn't it Aristotle who said not to be born is the best thing?" Dr. Irene Schmidt shifted her weight in the hospital bed. Her eyes were closed, her skin was gray, and her breathing spasmodic. "And death is better than life." Dr. Monroe choked as he stood by her bed in the hospital end of the compound, and tears flowed down his cheeks.

"Don't," he muttered.

"Don't what?" she breathed.

"Don't!"

"What you mean, dear Henry, is don't be naughty—don't die." Her voice was barely audible.

"Just . . . just take the chemotherapy as—"

"No chemotherapy," she said.

"It's your only chance."

"No," she whispered.

"Please," he said.

"It's just another experiment . . . I can't face another experiment," she murmured weakly.

"For my sake?"

"No—for *my* sake, I will not."

"How about for Sterling's sake?"

Her eyelids fluttered open. "Sterling?"

"He needs you!"

She gave a little coughing laugh. "Needs me? He's only three months old and he has two doctors and three nurses looking out for him!"

"But he needs you! He knows you now."

"The nurses will take excellent care of him."

"But he needs you. You are his mother."

"Mother!" She closed her eyes and smiled. "An honor I share with five other ladies. How many other women can make that statement? Henry . . . There is something I must tell you; something I've been meaning to tell you for some time . . ."

"Yes?"

"Sterling . . ."

"What about Sterling? He's a perfectly formed infant. He's immune to all disease. With his heritage he is bound to be imbued with great talents. Already his coordination seems to be precocious. I'm sure that ultimately he will be the super human being that Roosevelt and I planned—"

Dr. Schmidt raised herself up on one elbow. "Henry!" she said firmly. "Don't you realize? We have created this perfect human being . . . but God has given him a flaw!"

She began to choke.

"Darling . . ." he said. "What flaw?"

Irene gasped for breath and fell back against the pillows and closed her eyes. "He can't hear," she whispered. "He's deaf, do you understand, Henry, deaf . . ." She touched his hand. "Deaf," she repeated.

As Dr. Monroe stood speechless by her bedside holding her hand, she subsided into a coma and died two days later.

Dr. Henry Monroe left the compound two weeks later and returned to his Manhattan brownstone on Sixty-second Street. He arranged to have the child examined by the most outstanding specialists in the field, and Dr. Schmidt's suspicions regarding the infant's inability to hear were confirmed.

As time went on, Dr. Monroe was beginning to wonder how much longer he could continue to support his "project," for the original grant money was running out, and he had incurred unforeseen expenses. In addition to maintaining his household with its staff, he had hired a full-time nurse and companion for Sterling, Maxine, whose special training and remarkable gift for communicating with children had encouraged Dr. Monroe to believe that he could, after all, hope to see Sterling fulfill the tremendous expectations he had once had for his project.

Then one day as he was looking out the window, marveling at the wonderful rapport Sterling had with Maxine as they played "games" in the garden, the phone rang.

"White House calling for Doctor Monroe . . ."

A few minutes later, a midwestern twang announced, "Truman here."

"Yes, Mr. President."

"Doctor, you probably wondered why you've never heard from me, right?" There was a friendly chuckle on the other end of the phone.

"Well, I've been too busy learning how to be prezz-a-dent. Secondly, and now you're not going to believe this, but nobody ever told me about . . . well, you know what they never told me about! I'll let you know sometime how I finally found out. Let me tell you, sir, there are a lot of things I didn't know about. That the FBI didn't know about. That the OSS didn't know about. And hey, I don't want to say one damned word more on this subject because this phone is probably tapped. Now listen, Doctor, I think you've done one hell of a job from what I understand. I'd like to talk to you."

Dr. Monroe's mind reeled. For months he had considered what he would say in just this situation. Now that it was actually happening, he still felt unprepared as he replied, "Mr. President, I could, perhaps, come down next week sometime . . ."

"Tomorrow," said Truman bluntly.

"Tomorrow?"

"Noon," said Truman. "Oh, and listen . . . I don't understand diddly squat about the sort of thing you did here. Can you keep it simple?"

"It *is* simple, sir."

Dr. Monroe felt greatly heartened by the conversation. At last it had come, the moment when he would learn whether he had succeeded or failed in his assignment. He went again to the window and looked out at the child. Sterling was performing for Maxine and the doctor could tell by the look on her face that she was very pleased and proud of her protégé. Dr. Monroe would not hesitate to tell President Truman everything.

At the meeting Truman told Dr. Monroe that one million dollars had been placed in Sterling Mann's name. He was to be sent to the best schools in the United States, the best university in America, and the best graduate school in England. He was to be trained in the sciences, languages, ballistics, aerodynamics, weaponry, political science, cybernetics, the martial arts, and various athletic skills. He would, in short, become the ultimate, perfect agent awaiting only word from the President to go into action whenever a crisis of sufficient importance developed.

President Truman had thanked Dr. Monroe for his candor in revealing the problem that Sterling had and expressed admiration for the tremendous success Dr. Monroe had had in dealing with it. Sterling was able to function normally in every way. Thanks to Maxine, he had learned to communicate excellently, and thanks to his specially designed hearing aid, he was no longer handicapped. Dr. Monroe explained to the President the new developments in ear surgery with the use of the

operating microscope and promised that as soon
as the experiments proved successful, Sterling
would be given this advantage.

Any worry Dr. Monroe might have had was
bleached out by the years that went by. Thirty-
four years to be exact. Sterling had gone through
the toughest, most ingeniously planned education
and training that any man had ever been exposed
to, and he had completed it all with high honors.
He grew aware of what he was being trained for,
and he had a clear idea of what he wanted to do
in life until such time as he would be called upon
by the President.

At age ten the surgery that Dr. Monroe had so
earnestly hoped would solve Sterling's problem
had been performed, but Sterling was still de-
pendent upon an aid. His later interest in electronics undoubtedly stemmed from his curiosity about
Penelope, as he affectionately called his hearing
aid.

After his postgraduate studies were completed,
Sterling organized Mann Industries, Inc., a think
tank of young scientists and engineers with whom
Sterling had become acquainted during the various phases of his education and training. The or-
ganization was highly respected, and it developed
an enviable reputation for excellence as they
worked on revolutionary ideas and inventions for
the future. Mann Industries became a
multibillion-dollar operation, as the United States

government found Sterling's amazing inventions a
first-rate source for civilian and military projects.
Communication satellites, designed and con-
structed by Mann Industries, were placed in orbit—four of them in three years. And Sterling personally designed and perfected more than a
hundred new inventions and innovations which,
by the mid-eighties, would change many aspects
of the world.

Now that Sterling had appeared on the cover of
more than two dozen international magazines (he
made *Time* in the second year of Mann Industries'
existence) and had become one of the most cele-
brated scientists of the decade, Dr. Monroe had
no reason to worry about him anymore. His obli-
gation had been fulfilled. President Roosevelt's
dream had been realized. Perhaps the world of
super-spies was coming to an end. Perhaps the
only real danger that could threaten America now
was recession, depression . . . the economic cold
war. And Sterling was already serving his country
in that respect. Dr. Monroe had had no signs, in
over a decade, that the presidents of the United
States were even aware of Sterling's existence.
Could it be, he wondered a thousand times, that
somewhere along the line Sterling's heritage had
worn out? Could it be that "the ultimate American agent" had become a joke to those hard-nosed
pragmatists? Could it be that politicians' vision
had become so blurred by power and political ad-
vantage-seeking that they could see only the im-

mediate problems, those that surfaced before their
noses? As Dr. Monroe got older and as Sterling
became more famous, the pendulum that swung
above his head seemed to slow down. The gentle
old man thought of it at night when he went to
bed and quite often smiled to himself, almost sure
that Roosevelt had been a dreamer, a romantic,
and a lot of other things that could not survive in
the harsh political reality of the final decades of
the twentieth century.

He was happy that an earlier president hadn't
thought of using Sterling to blow up the Arabs to
terminate the energy crisis, especially since that
president had been ousted from the White House
in a rush and probably hadn't found time in all the
brouhaha to inform his successor about Sterling.
Considering the political turmoil that ensued, it
was not impossible that Sterling Mann had been
forgotten, like an old World War II air base or
an old Liberty ship.

CHAPTER FOUR

Oct. 10, 1982
7:02 A.M. Six hours after the
death of Alexandra Robinson
Place: Interstate 91, near Flagstaff, Arizona

The pretty woman was alone with her blue Ford
on the desolate landscape.

"Damn, damn, damn!" mumbled Melanie Ross.

She was petite, brown-haired, and while pretty,
not beautiful in any conventional way. At twenty-
eight she had at once a childlike quality to her
face and maturity beyond her age. She was vulnerable, yet able to cope, and two lines like com-
mas at the corners of her mouth indicated that she
smiled at life more than she frowned at it. But
now she'd lost patience. She was on her way to her

first vacation in years, a time with her glamorous older sister in New York that promised to be full of change and surprise and excitement, which she very much needed . . . and now this. Her lower lip pouted petulantly, and she looked like a little girl whose bike has broken down on the way to a birthday party. Hugging herself against the cold morning mist, she suddenly turned to the crippled car and childishly kicked once at its door.

She'd been waiting for what seemed like eons when she saw the strange vehicle loom over the horizon. At first it looked like an ordinary car . . . after all, it did have wheels. But as it drew closer, skimming over the gray ribbon of straight highway, she saw that it was wider in front than most cars and narrower in back and that it had a fin in the back almost like a plane's rudder.

It made a sinister hiss unlike any other automobile Melanie had ever heard—it sounded more like a cobra. The vehicle seemed to barely touch the asphalt, like a Hovercraft over water.

Melanie frantically held up her thumb, trying to move that digit seductively, but she gave up all hope when she realized how fast the vehicle was moving. It zoomed past her, a green blur, a streak. She lowered her arm.

Then, incredibly, it shifted down and screeched to a stop, then started to back up.

"The good news is that the guy stopped," she murmured to herself apprehensively as she watched the car approach. "The bad news is that he's Charlie Manson on parole."

The car was alongside her now, and the driver reached over and opened the door.

"Going my way, miss?" asked a deep, pleasant voice. She had expected a voice from Transylvania.

"What other way is there?" Melanie answered, bending down to look at the driver. He was not Charles Manson, that was obvious. He was incredibly good-looking—about thirty-three, dark brown hair, a tan that he'd apparently been born with. He was dressed immaculately in a short-sleeved sport shirt, gray slacks, and loafers. There was something different about him: His eyes. One was dark brown, the other blue.

"Do join me," he said softly.

It certainly wasn't an English accent, and it wasn't Boston Brahmin nor Locust Valley lockjaw. To Melanie it sounded like prep school, Ivy League with Cambridge or Oxford. And the biceps, not vulgarly engorged but very much there; they looked as though he might have stroked at Henley or backstroked at Yale or groundstroked at Wimbledon or . . .

She hauled out of her car a slightly beaten-up blue Samsonite suitcase and put it in the back of the car behind the seats. As she slid in beside him, he eased the machine into the first of seven gears; they moved very slowly and gently and then suddenly . . . they were going very, very fast.

"Leapin' lizards!" Melanie exclaimed.

"Does it bother you?" he asked.

"No. I always drive at a hundred and sixty miles an hour," she replied.

Every time either of them spoke, a row of tiny diodes, each no larger than the head of a pin, flickered across the dashboard over the speedometer out of Melanie's view.

The driver was smiling and silent until he said, "And you are . . . ?"

"Melanie Ross," she said and the diode lights traveled their green path across the dashboard.

"And what do you do, Melanie?" he asked politely.

"I'm a teacher for children with hearing disability," she said in her best headmistress voice, "the severely handicapped whose retardation is basically due to lack of functional hearing."

"Really!" he exclaimed, looking at the green lights.

He turned to her, genuine interest shining in his eyes. Then with his right hand he made the signs for: "I, too, know the language and am interested in those handicapped in that way."

"Oh, how do you happen to know signing?"

"I . . ." Sterling hesitated, then shrugged, "I was simply curious and thought it probably might be useful in some circumstance . . ." And the line of tiny diode lights shone red.

"And how are you on Swahili?" she said.

"Rusty," Sterling replied. Then glancing at his

watch, he frowned as if late for an appointment. "Where are you headed for?"

"To meet my husband," she said as a precautionary move against this too-handsome stranger. "He's waiting for me . . . in Flagstaff . . . must be wondering where I am."

The line of light went across the dashboard, but this time it was red again.

"I see," Sterling said, a smile barely cracking his lips once again.

The girl shifted her small frame as she changed the subject. Looking back over the car she asked, "German car?"

"It's an ESV, Experimental Safety Vehicle." He glanced at her now with a grin. "And since you always drive a hundred and sixty miles an hour, I presume you're accustomed to test rides like this. Even the windshield and windows are adapted for greater visibility and safety—they are made to become darker as the light increases and vice versa, just like the sunglasses that came out several years ago."

"And you, of course, are the genius who invented this wonder machine," she challenged. She didn't know why she felt so hostile toward this man who was doing her a favor and trying to be pleasant and amusing for her. He was just so . . . so damned perfect-looking . . . so attractive and interesting. There had to be something wrong. She had been very badly burned by a too-good-looking man a few years back. It was one of the reasons she had flung herself so totally into her work with the handicapped children and had built an iron curtain around her heart and emotions. The ego of good-looking men!

Sterling merely answered, "I'm still working out the bugs."

Suddenly Melanie became aware that the driver was slowing down very rapidly. She looked up and saw it in front of them at a distance of less than half a mile—a huge trailer-truck maneuvering across the highway.

As Sterling brought the ESV to a stop, he glanced at the five-inch television screen that replaced the usual rearview mirror and saw that another truck which had been behind them for the last two miles was closing in. As though that trouble were not enough, a thick cloud of white steam emerged from the truck in front of them and swirled about them like a dense fog. It was impossible to see the dark shapes that were now moving around the ESV. Sterling pressed the electronic alert button twice and an air-compressed horn sounded two piercing blasts. The dark figures, shrouded in the dense mist that soaked the windows, continued to move around them. Sterling pressed another button, and instead of conventional wipers, a stream of hot, dry air cleared the windshield. The figures were now well below his eye level. Solid steel bars had been inserted under the ESV and chains were attached to them. The silhouettes slipped into the fog again at the same time that Sterling shifted to low gear in an attempt to go over the shoulder of the road. Suddenly they heard the metallic clanking of heavy chains as they were tightening around the ESV. Sterling felt the jolt, but it was too late to react—the car was already being lifted off the ground by some unkown vehicle and being raised slowly but steadily out of the steam cloud.

Melanie looked at Sterling, apprehension written on her face. He said nothing but gave her what passed for a reassuring smile. Choking back the urge to scream, she asked, "I take it this is all part of your so-called 'test ride'?" Then she heard the chop-chop of the blades, and looking up, she could see the looming shape of a black helicopter.

"Something tells me they're not from Triple A," she said with a slight tremor in her voice.

The man behind the steering wheel beside her looked thoughtful—tense but not worried. He pressed a button and two heavy-duty saftety belts automatically strapped themselves around their bodies. He studied the instrument panel intently.

Melanie looked above as the huge black chopper took them up and up. Then when she looked down again, she gasped and froze, speechless as the shock of acrophobia engulfed her. They were over the Grand Canyon . . . high, high over the great fissures in the earth! Finding her voice, she heard herself say, "Is this what you call the 'overall' tour of the canyon?"

At that moment, with a great clanking of chains,

the helicopter released its cargo, and the front of
the car dipped as it started its dive. It was like a
fast elevator dropping out from under her. The
sudden movement held her in a thrall of catalepsy
as they went down and down.

The man quickly flipped a switch under the
panel. With a roar the engine came on, and at the
same time two exhausts just below the taillight
belched out a stream of thin bluish flame like an
acetylene torch from the twin eleven-thousand-
pound-thrust hydrogen peroxide rocket engines.
He eased the steering wheel toward his body and
the front of the car came up slowly. Next to the
hand brake was a lever, and as he yanked it up,
Melanie saw two stubby stabilizing flaps about
three feet long fan out from under the doors on
each side. He pressed a tiny button on the automatic gear shift and split it into two throttle levers. He pushed them forward and the roar of the
engine became louder. He tugged at the wheel,
and the car's front end evened off as it pulled out
forward, banking smoothly in the direction that
the helicopter had taken.

Melanie slumped in her seat, her face pale and
moist with the perspiration of relief as she mumbled, "You sure know how to liven up a girl's life."

In twenty seconds they caught up with the helicopter. They approached from under the belly of
the spiderlike craft with its empty chains trailing
like strands of web.

As they were closing in on the helicopter, Sterling pressed a button that caused the grill in front of the car to revolve and lock into place, making it now an oval-shaped microwave reflector. The driver lined up an etched circle in the windshield with the star-shaped radiator ornament, then gave a spurt of power to bring the nose up higher. When the helicopter was dead in his sights, his thumb pressed the red button on the top of the throttle. He fired twice, noiselessly.

Melanie saw the immediate effect of the microwave: The paint on the helicopter began to blister, and as the black peeled off, the silvery metal was revealed and then the steel and aluminum started to warp and melt and shrivel. As the crippled craft began its descent, she caught a glimpse of the expression of confusion and panic on the faces of the chopper's occupants. Sterling banked the car sharply away just before the aircraft exploded. He looked out the window to see the remains of the helicopter gyrate erratically down into the depths of the canyon below. It crashed on a ledge near the bottom of the chasm, and a great black cloud spiraled slowly upward.

Sterling pressed the button to roll back the microwave grill as he straightened the car up and headed in the opposite direction.

"The joy of cooking," Melanie muttered, shaking her head incredulously, and looking quite green-gray.

CHAPTER FIVE

Melanie Ross was still shaking from the helicopter experience when they came in low over the complex of buildings of Mann Industries east of Flagstaff in the flying car. Sterling banked the ESV around the high smokestack, reduced the jet power, and let the car down gently on the vast parking lot.

Once on the ground he pulled the lever that folded the stubby flaps, switched off the jets, and started the car's motor. He drove across the lot to the security guard's booth.

"Wow, Mr. Mann!" the young guard exclaimed. "I'd heard the rumors, but when you actually see that thing in action! Wow!"

Sterling grinned. "We're getting there. Say, Bill,

do me a favor, drive Miss Ross here any place she wants to go. I'm late for the meeting."

The guard looked at the pretty girl and smiled. "With pleasure, sir."

As Melanie got out of the car, Sterling said, "Thank you, Miss . . . er . . . Mrs. Ross."

"For what?"

"For being such good ballast . . . don't think we'd have made it otherwise."

Melanie replied, "Mother would have been pleased . . . she always wanted me to be a useful person."

"I hope we meet again, under less exciting circumstances," he said sincerely.

Knowing that it was useless to argue with a lunatic, Melanie smiled sweetly and nodded. But as he drove off, she muttered to herself, "Don't hold your breath."

The guard cleared his throat and Melanie realized he'd heard her and she felt guilty. Despite the fact that she had experienced seemingly a science-fiction episode over the Grand Canyon, close to what she surely felt must have been the end of her life, Melanie was not happy to see Sterling drive away. As the car ordered by the guard drove up and Melanie stepped into it, she turned to take a last look at the strange ESV. What had he called it? An experimental safety vehicle? Well named, as it certainly had brought her back alive. And he had designed it. What an incredible man!

But surely not one she would ever see again. And somehow Melanie felt grateful for that. A man that handsome and clever would not be interested in the dull sort that she was . . . a teacher of deaf children . . . she couldn't possibly have anything of common interest with such a man. Still, a wistful hope persisted in spite of all her rationalization.

Sterling gunned the car up a short ramp and into a tunnel in the side of the large building. In two minutes he was in the boardroom of Mann Industries and the ESV was turning on a revolving stage. Some hundred shareholders and board members applauded the spectacular car; it was their first look at one of the company's more dramatic products.

Sterling shook hands with several people as he got out of the car and strode to the podium.

"Thank you all," he said. "Of course, there are dozens of other people who worked on the ESV who deserve much of the credit. Besides its versatility, it is Mann Industries' contribution to the gas crisis, a situation which you all know seems only to worsen every year."

"What does the ESV use?" asked a gray-haired woman in the front row.

"The car uses a combination of power. Essentially, I took an improved solar converter and combined it with a revolutionary oxygen burner.

Yes, just oxygen out of the atmosphere. The result is great horsepower and absolutely no pollution, and it is very inexpensive to operate."

"Is it true that the car actually flies?" asked a man.

"It flies," replied Sterling, "but we don't have sufficient horsepower for it to take off by itself. However, once it is launched from a high ramp or—" he took a deep breath—"or say, a helicopter, it flies like a dream."

"Amazing!" said a board member. "Has it been tested then?"

Sterling smiled ruefully. "Just a short while ago."

Dr. Monroe, now white-haired and white-bearded, frowned and said gruffly from his front-row seat, "I thought you agreed to let a test pilot fly it first."

"Doctor Monroe, I had little option in the matter," Sterling replied and shifted the topic. "Now, another product . . . a progress report on our holographic work. As you know, this has been a pet of ours, a favorite toy, if you will. But we are beginning to see some practical uses for it. For example . . ."

He held up a small device, no bigger than a pack of cigarettes. "This, in a few years, may revolutionize the TV industry. It could also change some military concepts. Let me tell you about this magic. It is widely known that holography, the projection of three-dimensional images, requires bulky equipment—laser sources which consume a lot of power and are difficult to operate. More important, those laser illusions are not moving pictures, just images which change and seem to move only when the angle of viewing changes. We took the principal of laser-projected holographic images and condensed it into tomorrow's electronics. In this miniature projector there are some elements that will transform our life in the eighties. The laser beam projector has been replaced by a light intensifier, the size of a penlight battery. This marvelous unit multiplies the existing light by two hundred thousand times, replacing the expensive, bulky laser light source. Furthermore, we have managed to eliminate the spun plastic material onto which conventional holography must project the laser image."

Some people in the audience looked confused.

"Information that, up to now, would necessarily have been stored in film or on magnetic tape, here takes up no more space than a fingernail, because we are using the new storing system of picture and sound-digital recording. Finally, we utilized the silicon chip that will some day replace the conventional TV tube. So here it is, ladies and gentlemen, the first holographic projector in a cigarette pack."

He placed the device on the stand and smiled.

"It even carries the warning, 'May be hazardous to your health.'"

The door behind him burst open and three men

dressed in uniforms and armed with machine guns ran out into the auditorium. Short bursts of fire shattered the quiet of the room, and stunned faces turned pale as people ducked or threw themselves on the floor. The sound of bullets ricocheting off the walls and screams filled the air, barely audible over the havoc the machine guns spread.

Sterling remained calm and smiling. He pressed a button on the projector, and the soldiers froze. The sound died instantly and Sterling walked over to the terrorists—and through them.

"I'm sorry to have frightened you," he said as the audience collected itself. "I thought after a boring scientific lecture some dramatic action might illustrate the effectiveness of our device in the best possible way."

A Pentagon man in a gray suit sighed.

"Now you have seen that one can barely tell real people from holographic images. That means that the long awaited dream of sending imaginary soldiers to the battle could now come true. In a few years a whole army filmed in a Hollywood back lot could be projected via satellite anywhere in the world in full realistic three-dimensional scale. An army that can appear and disappear at the command of a remote control, create confusion, delays, havoc, and panic while the enemy tries to figure out which are the real soldiers and which are the holographs."

He touched the projector again and the three human images disappeared.

"Well, unless anyone has some further questions, I'll just say thank you for coming and for being part of our family. Good day and we'll see you next month."

As the audience applauded, Sterling walked over to Dr. Monroe, took him warmly by the arm, and they walked together toward Sterling's office. On the way he told the doctor about the helicopter incident, concluding with a shake of his head, "All this training was for nothing . . . I was scared up there!"

Dr. Monroe patted his arm. Then he frowned. "Who could it have been?"

"By the process of elimination," said Sterling, "it quite possibly might have been the Arabs, or it could have been some competitor in the car business."

"Why do you rule out the possibility of agents from another country?"

"My identity is reasonably secure—other than you and the President, nobody knows. To get me, it only takes a telescopic rifle or any other lethal weapon. The whole caper with the helicopter points to another direction."

"Perhaps you're right. Perhaps your cover has become more dangerous to you than your identity as an agent. Perhaps they were after you and the ESV at the same time. The Arabs?"

"A car on the market that uses just oxygen instead of fossil fuels could harm a lot of people—

not just the Arabs. Next time they move in, we'll
see."

Dr. Monroe didn't like the sound of it. "Maybe
we should give you some company."

"A security guard?" Sterling smiled. "Hardly."

The answer Dr. Monroe expected. Sometimes
he thought he got trapped in his own personal
feelings for Sterling and forgot that this man—so
civilized-looking on the surface—could decimate a
small army single-handedly. Because Sterling
Mann, the inventor, the businessman, the coveted
one of jet set society, was the perfect combination
of physical strength and superior intelligence,
qualities backed by a high degree of ethical stam-
ina that gave his most trivial gadgetry a status
worthy of consideration.

Sterling timed his flight from Kennedy Airport.
It was six minutes and forty-one seconds. The
time was five forty-seven, just before dusk, when
the two-seater jet ranger helicopter settled down
smoothly on the small heliport in the middle of
tall fully grown cypress and palm trees. The miniature forest took up almost half the space of his
New York penthouse and was another of Mann Industries' minor miracles. An electronic control of
humidity and temperature connected to the
plants' roots made this magnificent garden possible regardless of New York weather conditions.

The rotor died and the blades spun slowly to a
stop. Nicholas Meyers, an aging Englishman with

side chops and pink cheeks, came out to greet them.

Sterling had a soft spot for tradition, and although he sometimes had an urge to revolutionize anything that was a classic or a cliché, he did like an English butler and a vintage English car.

Sterling shook his hand and Dr. Monroe patted Nicholas on the back.

"How goes it, old chum?" Dr. Monroe said teasingly with a fake English accent.

It took Nicholas a few seconds to reply, "Very-well-thank-you-sir."

His voice came with an electronic stutter. Dr. Monroe turned, surprised, and saw that Nicholas was punching buttons on a small hand-held computer.

"Nicholas had a blister on his vocal cords," said Sterling.

"Me-no-talk-two-seven-days," said Nicholas with his electronic voice, and Dr. Monroe shook his head in admiration.

"That one of your gadgets, Sterling?" asked Dr. Monroe as they walked toward the French doors.

"It's been around for a while . . . vocabulary of some hundred and seventy-five words," said Sterling. "Oh, and Nicholas, please bring some champagne to celebrate the inaugural flight of the ESV."

"Splendid idea!" said Mr. Monroe as they stepped into the living room. It was beautifully furnished, from the Aubusson rug to the coroman-

del screen—the big Monet of the Seine, the little
Vuillard of the Bois, the antique furniture. Over
the fireplace a portrait by Pène du Bois of Dr. Irene
Schmidt done posthumously from photos looked
down lovingly; she was the woman Sterling had
always believed to be his real mother. His father,
he had been told, was killed in a plane crash when
he was one year old. He knew Dr. Monroe as his
mother's brother.

"Let me show you an interesting new thing,"
said Sterling. He walked over to the elegant
Queen Anne cabinet, pulled open a drawer, and
touched an invisible thermo-electric switch. Silently the tapestry slid sideways on the east wall,
and there it was, a huge, flat television screen.

Dr. Monroe was not impressed; he had seen
that screen before and knew that it was one inch
thick and operated on a gas discharge panel.

Dan Rather was announcing an interview with
the President, and as soon as his picture came on
the screen, Sterling activated the voice stress analyzer, which accurately measured the tremor of
the vocal cords, a sign of someone lying.

Monroe tried to hide his smile as the lights at
the bottom of the screen traveled from left to
right in red.

"You didn't bring me here to show me that he
lies," said Dr. Monroe. "All politicians lie."

Sterling smiled and walked to the cabinet in the
corner of the room. He took a conventional-

looking digital watch from a drawer and slipped the bracelet around his wrist.

"No," he said. "I wanted you to be here for this premiere." He pressed a tiny switch on the watch. CBS's evening news disappeared from the large screen, and a rapid burst of digital and numerical characters flashed on the silver background.

"Good evening, sweetheart," Sterling said softly.

The digital writing formed instantly a series of words: "Good evening, Sterling. How are things?"

"You repaired Penelope!" Dr. Monroe exclaimed.

"Not only repaired . . . improved, Doctor Monroe," said the writing on the wall. "I feel like new."

"Amazing!"

"Thank you," replied the digital writing.

"You see," Sterling said, "she has been my long and painful labor of love for years. But now she is perfect."

Nicholas walked in with a bottle of champagne and two chilled glasses.

Sterling filled one glass and lifted it toward the screen. "Here's to you, girl," he said. "And to the ESV . . . two premieres in one day."

The words traveled fast across the screen: "You . . . are drinking champagne?"

Sterling gave the screen a friendly smile and said, "I am just making the toast. Doctor Monroe is drinking the champagne."

Dr. Monroe brought the glass to his lips, unable to take his eyes off the screen. "How much did it cost?" he asked.

"Twenty-four million."

"Are you going to tell the Pentagon?"

"Penelope is the most advanced computer of the century. She is programmed with an overload of knowledge . . . Everything I know and a lot that I don't know. I am not giving her to any Pentagon."

"He is very possessive," noted Penelope on the screen.

"As you can see, she even has a sense of humor," said Sterling, filling a glass with Evian water. "It's the advantage of creating a computer that stores information in tiny nitrogen bubbles. It takes one thousand times less space and leaves you room for some personality traits—sense of humor, understanding, female idiosyncrasies, and a controlled individuality that allows her to make decisions in difficult moments."

He glanced up at the portrait of Irene Schmidt. "And she is a loving, caring woman, like Mother."

"Fascinating. Is she linked?"

"Oh, yes. She can transmit or receive in a nanosecond anywhere in the world . . . and beyond."

He held up his wrist to show Dr. Monroe the watch.

Dr. Monroe put on his half glasses and tried to focus on the tiny screen. The digital display on the watch showed the time and date. Sterling pushed a button and the readout shifted to tiny words that traveled rapidly across the four-millimeter window. "You see, Doctor Monroe, I come in all shapes and sizes," Penelope said in her digital writing.

Sterling explained to Dr. Monroe what he was already suspecting. When Mann Industries sold their last communications satellite to the U.S. government, they not only designed the announced improvements that made Century Star the biggest and most perfect relay station, they also reserved a unique high-frequency channel for Penelope. No one but Sterling could use the transmit-receive coordinates of this channel. And no one but Penelope could be linked with this channel to provide her "master" with instant information wherever he was.

"But what about the voice function?" asked Dr. Monroe, his eyes still transfixed on the watch. "Isn't it a handicap to have to speak actually, physically to the computer? What do you do when you are in front of other people?"

Sterling enjoyed this shrewd observation. Though the doctor was getting old, he hadn't lost his mental acuity.

He pointed at the silver-plated sensor on the back of the wrist terminal. "You recognize that, of course."

Dr. Monroe nodded. He had initiated that sensor—a translator of sound into electrical current, the unit that helped Sterling "hear" for the first time. It was primitive and bulky in the beginning, but later Sterling had miniaturized it into a wristwatch. The "sensor" was an amplifier and microphone condensed in one; it could pick up sounds and voices, transform them to electrical current of low voltage and high amperage, and send it, through nerve impulse, directly to Sterling's brain. Simulated hearing, very effective and efficient. But what did it have to do with the computer?

Sterling explained that Penelope could talk to him through his hearing device, since Penelope could talk directly in electrical current.

"Yes, yes," said Dr. Monroe impatiently, "but how do *you* communicate with her whenever you can't talk?"

"I just think. It is an improvement in the speculation in cybernetics . . . to link a human brain with a computer."

Signs of concern became etched around Dr. Monroe's eyes as he asked, "You didn't do anything dangerous, did you?"

Sterling placed the watch back on his wrist. "If you are asking me whether I planted electrodes in my brain . . . no . . ." He tapped his finger on the watch. "Everything is done right here," he said. "And it is fairly simple. The 'watch' contains a miniature SQUID, a superconducting quantum interference device. The most sensitive ever produced. The SQUID generates a very accurate encephalogram, which Penelope, through a built-in 'intelligence amplifier,' translates into digital information. You simply think . . . she understands."

Dr. Monroe shook his head thoughtfully. As a scientist, he felt envious; as a creator, proud, and yet something was troubling him. He continued to look at the watch as he said, "It seems that all of the effort that went into the attempt to create a perfect human being has resulted only in the creation of another machine . . . a very sophisticated human substitute . . . complete with endearing human qualities. Perhaps I'm an old fool." Monroe shrugged. "Here I am, looking at the world's most amazing toy, and I keep thinking, why build it . . . why not continue to rely on human intelligence?"

Sterling put his arm around his uncle's shoulder. Then he smiled, "*Nescis, filius meus, quantilla sapientia regitur mundus.*"

And Penelope's translation came immediately: "You will never know, my son, with what real knowledge the world is run."

Dr. Monroe nodded and chuckled. "Or as a hack playwright once penned, 'There are more things in heaven and earth, Horatio, than are dreamt of in your philosophy' . . . I suspect that is truer now than back in old Will's day!"

Sterling laughed, relieved, and said, "That must be the same character who said, 'There's a destiny that shapes our ends, rough-hew them how we may!' "

Dr. Monroe agreed. "Yes, I suppose the last

'Master of his fate' went down with the last sailing ship."

Sterling then pointed out, "Since she never has to powder her nose or take a coffee break, our Penelope never fails to answer the telephone and relay the messages."

"You could say that I am a girl friday," came the writing on the screen.

"Do you have any messages for Sterling?" asked Dr. Monroe. Penelope did not respond to his voice; instead WTK appeared on the screen and flashed for a second.

"What the hell is that?" he asked.

Sterling smiled. "Protection against any attempt to bug Penelope. Although she responds to other voices in making conversation, she is only programmed to answer my questions—a voice-identification sensor. That WTK stands for 'Who's to know?'—less formal than 'Insufficient data.'"

Then he turned and spoke to the screen. "Do you have any messages for me, sweetheart?"

"I swear," muttered Dr. Monroe, shaking his head. "A man having a love affair with his computer!"

The sound of recorded messages was fed into clear hi-fi loudspeakers. A phone call from Paul Newman, saying he would be in town next Tuesday. A message from the William Morris agency with an invitation to the world premiere of Bob Fosse's new musical.

And then Alexandra Robinson's voice wavered

statically over the speakers: "I've got to talk to you! Just got back from Europe and have a story that will make World War II look like a Fourth of July picnic—but I need to use your computer."

Then the second call: "Sterling, for God's sake . . . I'm sure I'm being followed and I'm scared to death . . . black Cadillac . . . going to make a run for it . . . will try to get back to you . . ."

Immediately after that, Penelope played the third and final call: "Your damn machine again!" Alexandra's voice was distorted and metallic. "I know they're after me . . . I think I'm safe for the moment . . . I'm at Equinox on Fifty-fourth Street . . . try to come here if you return in time . . ."

"Lord!" Sterling said. "That doesn't sound good."

"Alexandra Robinson? Miss TV herself? A girl of yours?"

While Dr. Monroe was firing those questions, Sterling was already on the phone, punching Alexandra's number on the Touch-Tone dial.

The phone rang and rang . . . no answer. Just then Nicholas walked in and put the New York *Daily News* on the cocktail table.

"Heard-call-see-this," he said in computerese.

Sterling looked at the paper and put down the phone.

He didn't touch it. He simply read the headline, saying, " 'Alexandra Robinson—dead from drugs.' "

Dr. Monroe grabbed the paper and read aloud.

"It says, 'Famed TV personality dies mysteriously at Equinox disco. Cocaine and liquor most likely cause.' "

Dr. Monroe studied Sterling's face. Beneath the calm, controlled surface, he could see the struggle to keep that cool visage. Sterling's eyes had an almost liquid darkness and a vein on his temple was swollen as he stared out the panoramic window. Finally he said softly, "I might have been able to help her . . . if only I had checked with Penelope late last night. I made my last check-in about five P.M. which would be eight o'clock here. Then, today there was so much going on out there in Arizona . . ." He added with a somewhat shaken voice, "I'm going to the morgue now, would you like to come along and play Watson?"

CHAPTER SIX

It had taken them one hour and forty minutes to complete what to a coroner would have been an infinitely complicated task. There was no problem getting in to view the body. It lay in a brightly lit room with twenty other draped forms awaiting autopsy the next day. The attendant had drawn back the sheet, and Sterling winced as he saw Alexandra's gray face and parted lips, pretty even in death. The face and body appeared to be unblemished.

Slowly Sterling passed his wristwatch over the brown hair, the neck, the breasts, and the various parts of the nude body. The attendant had no way of knowing that Penelope, through her remote terminal, was scanning Alexandra's body, recording every bit of data they would need later on.

Now, back at the penthouse, Sterling and Dr.

Monroe were sitting silently in front of the large screen, with the fireplace crackling, waiting for Penelope to work out the information.

Sterling felt his mouth dry and bitter. The memory of Alexandra, that explosive source of energy and intelligence, lying cold and dead on the operating table at the morgue had upset him physically and he felt nauseated. He was sure the nausea, a sensation almost unknown to him, was subliminal guilt. He tried to shake it off, but Alexandra's face kept coming back in a succession of images: Alexandra smiling, Alexandra talking on the TV screen, Alexandra lying dead.

When the IAR sign flashed on the screen, Penelope's signal for "I am ready," Sterling asked her to give them a rundown on all the available facts.

Dr. Monroe studied them silently and then said, "The way Penelope reconstructs the death—well, it looks like a bizarre murder. First of all, rule out the cocaine-alcohol theory. Looks like motor paralysis followed by respiratory failure."

"The first thing that comes to my mind is a poison . . ." Sterling shrugged. "Something like curare, perhaps?"

"How? In a drink . . . ?"

Sterling asked Penelope to run the chart of the body again. As she was performing a one to one hundred magnification on the scalp, Sterling noticed the small irregularity even before Penelope could record it.

"There!"

Penelope froze the image.

"Make it one to a thousand."

The magnification now showed clearly that it was indeed a wound. Sterling asked for Penelope's data on the wound and the digital readout came back: "To make this wound, the object causing same would have to come from above . . . an object striking her cranium at about a 120° angle."

"A flying object with poison on it . . . a dart?" mused Dr. Monroe.

"It doesn't look like a dart wound," said Sterling.

In a more powerful magnification he was proved to be right. The wound looked more like a bite.

Neither spoke for a moment. Then Dr. Monroe said, " 'Course we could be wrong. We will find out a lot more tomorrow after the autopsy. Meanwhile, I think I'll go home and collapse. You, too, fellow. You take care of yourself."

Sterling took him to the elevator and came back with a question that Penelope had already anticipated.

"What kind of bite?"

She ran through the charts of almost five hundred bites from insects to small monkeys. The field was finally narrowed down to two possibilities: A marmoset or a bat—and since it was a scalp wound, Sterling was certain that it was the bite of a bat, most likely a fully grown vampire bat.

He began to get the picture: A wound from

above. Curare. Was it possible that a poisoned bat had been used to kill Alexandra? But how had the bat been guided to Alexandra—and no one else in that room?

It was Penelope who came up with a feasible possibility. "A bat trained to get its food by responding to an electronic guiding signal would then go to anyone wearing a similar electronic device."

Penelope also threw a question at Sterling: "But why would Alexandra wear such a device?"

"Elementary, my dear Penelope," Sterling said. "Planted on her."

Then he had a sudden thought . . . "How would you compare the origins and motives of this murder with the attempt against me today?"

Penelope flashed a WTK and Sterling smiled faintly. She hadn't been fed any data on that morning's episode.

As he got up, ready to leave, Penelope wondered on the screen: "Where are you going?"

"I'm going over to Alexandra's apartment," he said. "Let you take a look and see what you can find."

"Be careful," the computer read. "You might be followed."

"Who's to know?" countered Sterling as he strode to the elevator.

Penelope watched, with her thoughtful electronic eye, as Sterling entered the elevator and descended to the street level until she could no longer see him. But she had all the necessary data from his wrist terminal, and she knew he was calm and cool because the readouts from the thin sensor plate touching his skin were constant. Penelope could tell at any moment his body temperature, his perspiration rate, pulse, and blood pressure . . . she could even identify his skin tissue type. When fifteen minutes later he parked the Silver Cloud convertible in front of the building at 1054 Fifth Avenue, Penelope knew that she had been there before. Even though it was at a previous stage of her existence, the memory cells that contained information from her embryonic stage before Sterling had redesigned her told her this was not the first time.

"Evenin', Mr. Mann," said the Jamaican doorman as he opened the door of the elegant apartment building.

"Bloody shame 'bout Miss Alexandra, weren't it?"

"It certainly was, Jess."

"Nice lady, that."

"The nicest," Sterling agreed as he hurried to the elevator.

"Say, Mr. Mann!" Jess called after him, but Sterling was already in the elevator and the doors were closing. The doorman shrugged.

On the fourth floor, Sterling quickly went to apartment 4B. It was locked.

"Got a lock here . . . can you open it for me?" he asked the portable Penelope.

"Alien presence," she warned.

Just then the door of an adjacent apartment opened and a Puerto Rican maid stepped out in the hall.

"*Buenas noches*," said Sterling, pleasantly. "*Todo va bien?*"

The girl smiled. "*Muy bien*," she answered, picking up the evening paper and stepping back inside.

"The lock," Sterling said.

"The pin tumbler lock was invented by Linus Yale in 1848, who then went on to—"

"Open it!" Sterling commanded.

"Yes, sir," Penelope replied. "Hold me close to it."

Sterling held the wrist terminal against the doorknob. Penelope scanned it with infrared sensors, emitted three different electric currents that created an effective magnetic field, and the door clicked open.

"Thanks," he whispered.

Carefully he opened the door. The apartment was dark and he stepped cautiously into the living room. Penelope was more comfortable in the dark as she could "see" with her infrared sensors. As he moved around the furniture, using his sixth sense as his guide, his eyes adjusted quickly, and he could now see quite well in the dark. It would have taken an average human ten times longer to adapt his vision to the lack of light.

He went to the bedroom and slipped in. A fraction of a second before Penelope emitted the buzzing warning of an alien presence, Sterling knew and had already turned to face the assailant.

In the next instant Sterling grabbed the hand holding the poker and spun, flinging his assailant over his head. He heard the body fall on the bed with a cry . . . a feminine cry. He snapped on the light and stared in disbelief.

Melanie Ross was lying on the bed, holding her aching wrist.

"Melanie!" Totally baffled, he looked down at her, dressed in a filmy nightgown . . . the girl he'd left in Arizona earlier in the day. "What are you doing here?"

"You son of a bitch," she gasped. "How did you get in? And just what are *you* doing in my sister's apartment?"

Her sister's apartment? Alexandra . . . her sister?

He managed to control his surprise immediately. "I'm looking for clues," he said.

"Clues! Don't tell me you're the police, 'cause I'll be damned if I'll swallow that!"

"No, not really. But I feel obliged to do what I can in this case. Alexandra was a friend of mine. She once did a very fine piece on Mann Industries . . . during all the interviewing we became good friends. And when I got back today, there were several messages from her indicating that she was in some kind of trouble. Then, of course, you know what happened . . ."

Melanie looked at him, unconvinced. "Wow, what a day! First the Buck Rogers act, and now here you are sneaking around my sister's apartment 'looking for clues.' So what are you? A bored, screwy millionaire who likes to play Inspector Clouseau?"

He didn't answer but sat down on the bed, his eyes indicating to Melanie that she, too, had some explaining to do. "She never told me she had a sister," he said.

"Well, she had one. My sister . . ." She suddenly gave a little sob.

Then Melanie sat back on the bed, and the tears came quickly as she blew her nose in the already wet handkerchief. Sterling reached over and put his arm around her shoulders. She spoke slowly and haltingly between occasional snuffles and long pauses.

"When you found me out there on the highway this morning, I was on my way to the airport to spend my vacation with Alexandra. She phoned me yesterday to confirm my arrival and said she had so much to tell me and she sounded so excited. Being older, she was always so concerned with my career . . . almost like a mother would have been. Ours died when I was a young child. And Alex's life was so glamorous compared to mine. Physically, we were not the closest of sisters . . . we were too different. But we were good friends. You know, of course, that she had married and was divorced. That's why our last names are different."

Melanie continued, "I could hardly wait to see Alex again. Then I get here and find she's dead! And, oh, God, cocaine? I can't believe that . . . someone must have forced it on her . . . maybe you." She looked at him accusingly. "She wouldn't kill herself."

"I don't think she did kill herself," Sterling said.

"But who would want to kill her?"

Sterling asked, "When did you last talk to her?" He got up and started looking around in the various drawers.

Melanie told him about her last telephone conversation before yesterday's. It contributed nothing that he didn't already know, but he continued to probe and made her repeat it.

She followed him as he went into the study.

"But where in Europe had she been?" he asked.

"She didn't say . . . just Europe."

"Europe's a rather large place," said Sterling, walking over to the large desk in the center of the room.

He began leafing through the papers—half-finished articles, interviews, clippings, fan letters, hate mail, photographs. The big, cluttered desk seemed still to pulsate, for it had been the heart of Alexandra's life. Sterling could not find anything that seemed significant and Penelope confirmed this.

He checked the typewriter. In it was a sheet of paper with the title, "Those Naughty Ladies Behind the Scenes in Washington." He scanned it, then his eye fell upon the pad next to the telephone. The top page had been torn off. Sterling cursed progress and all its disadvantages; had it not been for the soft marker pen, had a pencil or ballpoint been used, he could have made out the notes from the marks left etched into the surface of the page beneath it. He went back to the typewriter, her "steady boyfriend" as she used to call it—an IBM Magnetic Card. He reached for the type button and pressed it. The machine spanned two spaces and started typing fast.

Melanie watched. But after a moment, Sterling pressed the stop button; the article had nothing of interest to him. He looked around and spotted the small gray box with the magnetic cards stored in it. He removed the one in the machine and inserted another. Again the IBM spat letters on a fresh sheet of paper. Again nothing relevant to Alexandra's murder. Then, on the fourth disc, Sterling's eyes widened slightly as the machine typed out rapidly:

> MEMO: TO MYSELF
> BEFORE LEAVING
> DON'T FORGET
> HAIR AT 10
> CALL MIKE
> TICKETS PA 380 RAM 40

He took the page out. "She booked two flights," he said. "Pan Am three-eighty . . . where to, girl?"

Melanie was about to reply when she realized Sterling was talking to his wristwatch. Penelope recorded the question and the answer came back in a second: "PA Flight three-eighty to Rome via Casablanca."

Melanie forced a little smile as she watched Sterling talking to Penelope on his wristwatch terminal and said with a head shake of incredulity, "Now we get the Dick Tracy act."

"Then," Sterling was saying, "she probably took Royal Air Maroc's flight forty."

"Departing Monday, Wednesday, Friday, fifteen twenty, to Marrakesh," Penelope added, as if proud of her efficiency.

Marrakesh. Strange, although he'd gone to Oxford with the prince, Alī Moullah, and had seen him and the princess since in London, Paris, and Tangiers, he'd never before been to Marrakesh to accept their open invitation to visit them.

He looked at Melanie. He faintly recalled Alexandra's telling him that her parents were dead but asked Melanie, "Do you have anyone that you can call who would be able to help you with the arrangements?"

Melanie looked down and for a moment Sterling thought that she might cry, but then she said firmly, "Alex and I were alone, we had no other family and both our parents have been dead for some time. I am quite used to taking care of things myself."

"Let me help," Sterling offered. "Alexandra was my good friend and I would like to be your friend if you will let me."

Melanie started to say, "Thank you, but I really—"

"You must also realize that you cannot stay here in your sister's apartment. Whoever killed her may not have got what he wanted. I suspect it was information connected with her job. Anyway, this place is surely not safe for you. I really think you should get dressed and come with me."

"Where to?" she asked.

"To my apartment."

She eyed him suspiciously.

"It's a very big apartment," he said with a broad smile.

They came out of the building, and as Jess held open the door of Sterling's car, he explained that he had tried to let him know that Melanie was there. Sterling gave him a tip, thanked him, and drove off. Neither Sterling, nor Melanie, not even the observant doorman noticed that a dark green Range Rover with tinted glass moved slowly after the Rolls.

Behind the wheel was the fat Englishman. He still wore his enigmatic smile, but he was no longer costumed as a ringmaster. Instead he was nattily dressed in a suit from Poole's and a hom-

burg. He apparently did not have the little mirrored cage with him. However, on the seat beside
him was a transparent florist's box with two beautiful golden orchids—with three large mosquitoes
nested in the deep tubular lips frilled with russet.

Sterling's transatlantic flight to Casablanca was
not scheduled to leave until noon, so he and Melanie had a breakfast of eggs Benedict on the terrace of the penthouse. A striped umbrella shielded
them from the morning sun of a glorious sum-
merlike day. The newspapers had been put
away by the caring Nicholas; the headlines about
Alexandra's death could upset Melanie. For the
same reason the TV was switched off, since the
networks had preempted their regular program-
ming in order to play Alexandra's tapes, her contro-
versial interviews, and investigations of her tragic
death.

Sterling tried to make pleasant conversation,
but it was difficult to distract Melanie from the
shock of her sister's murder, or even to dissuade
her from the notion that she should actively in-
volve herself in solving the crime. She was still in-
timidated and frightened by Sterling's charm, and
especially his reliance on assorted new electronic
equipment; she was accustomed to dealing with
problems on a one-to-one basis, as one who dealt
with handicapped children would naturally do, so
she was ready to cope with all other problems in a
similar manner. The tensions that were later to
plague the relationship between Melanie and Ster-

ling were based on this difference in approach to life's problems, but the difference also enabled each to at least consider others ways of assessing things. Of course, it made for conflict, but it also enhanced the odds for success as various problems arose.

Sterling was pleased that Melanie got on well with Nicholas; she hadn't failed to notice the fresh carnation at her place setting. When Melanie inquired about his talking device, she was much intrigued, and later said, "A thing like that would be marvelous for some of my deaf-mute students."

"You seem interested . . . would you care to see my workshop?" Sterling offered.

Melanie's curiosity overpowered her misgivings and she nodded.

They went into a large room filled with wheels and coils and transformers and blueprints and dozens of other objects that Melanie had never seen and of which she couldn't begin to guess the purpose.

"My playpen," he said with a smile. "My toys."

"If I'm supposed to be impressed, I am. What's that oversized egg, something else you're hatching?"

"That oversized egg is a bathing device. See, it opens like this, you step in, and it will automatically enfold your body while your head sticks out the top. Then a warm shower starts, followed by ultrasonically activated bubbles that cleanse the skin thoroughly but very gently. Then comes a whirling current of rinse containing special moisturizers and emollients for the skin. After that, small rubber balls buffet the entire body in a stimulating massage as the water drains out and low-moisture warm air circulates to dry you perfectly."

"Ooh, I love it!" Melanie exclaimed. "But it would never fit in *my* bathroom."

Just as they returned to the living room, Dr. Monroe suddenly appeared at the French doors.

"Sterling, so glad I caught you before you left," he said as he approached. "Just came from the autopsy. It was all just as we suspected. Murder . . . curare!"

Curare? Sterling mused to himself. But how come it didn't kill the bat? That was something he'd have to discover.

Sterling and Dr. Monroe walked out to the helicopter pad on the terrace.

"Sterling, are you sure you must do this thing? Tearing off this way, getting embroiled?"

"Sometimes," said Sterling, "I get the impression that you don't want to accept the fact that I was trained to be an agent."

"A very expensive one," affirmed Dr. Monroe. "You shouldn't take risks without an order . . . or even consent."

Dr. Monroe was simply worried about his "child's" safety. As the years passed, he had managed to forget that Sterling was not his real son . . . only his creation. In either case the burden of responsibility for Sterling's existence did not rest lightly upon him, and Sterling was touched by the old man's concern.

Melanie came up to them outside. "Since Alexandra was *my* sister, I do not understand why you will not let me go with you. I can pay my own way, and surely there must be something I could do to help."

"I appreciate how you feel, Melanie," Sterling replied. "But I must ask you to stay here. Besides, there's the funeral to attend. And as much as I would like to be there with you, I think I owe it more to Alexandra to unravel this mystery. Doctor Monroe will see to it that all the proper arrangements are made."

"You realize that you can't keep me here against my will," she said.

"Of course not, but I hope you'll stay here until I get back."

Dr. Monroe interceded, saying, "It is truly only for your own safety. Please try to understand that."

Melanie lowered her eyes but said nothing. Then Sterling leaned forward and gave her a brief kiss on the forehead.

She looked up at him for an instant, gave him a grudging smile, and said, "Bon voyage," in a wistful tone. Their two-day acquaintance made him her oldest friend in New York, and now he was leaving.

Sterling climbed into the helicopter and raised

his hand in a brief good-bye as the craft lifted off the pad and pointed toward the airport. She was a game little thing, he thought, kindly, not so brashly confident as her sister but certainly as brave. He almost wished he could bring her along . . . but it was too risky. He had no idea what he might find or even if there were anything in Marraskesh that had to do with Alexandra's death. But he had to start somewhere.

He had checked with the airlines, and everything seemed to confirm that Alexandra Robinson had indeed been in Marrakesh. Prince Ali Moullah could help him contact the most likely sources of information, and while the prince knew his background to be that of an inventor, he would appreciate Sterling's concern for Alexandra as a friend.

Yes, Marrakesh would be the best place to start.

The staccato of the blades had barely died in the distance when the bell rang.

Nicholas took a look at the television screen and saw a delivery boy standing in front of the elevator door. He pushed the up button, and in a few seconds he was standing in front of the butler, being scrutinized.

"Delivery for Miss Ross," he said.

Nicholas took the florist's box, gave the boy fifty cents, ignored the boy's disappointment, and took the box to Melanie's room.

Melanie stayed out on the terrace long after Sterling's helicopter had blended into the distant

haze. She stared resentfully out over the city that
had killed her sister. She gave a little shiver as the
sensation of loneliness and helplessness engulfed
her. She had looked forward to this visit with Alexandra, had tried to imagine all the things they
would do—the shopping, the matinees, the parties
at which she would be meeting many of the exciting people who were Alexandra's friends. Now all
she had to look forward to was the funeral . . .
and her final farewell.

Dr. Monroe came out onto the terrace and went
over to Melanie. "My dear," he said, "I know how
you must feel. I have just come from the kitchen,
where Nicholas and I decided that we'd give you
dinner at home. Sterling asked me to do what I
thought best in that matter. Now I must go out for
a while to take care of some things at my place,
but I shall return to have dinner with you."

Melanie gave him a grateful smile. She had
quite forgotten how kind and thoughtful some
men could be.

"You needn't do that, Doctor Monroe. I'll be all
right," Melanie said, not very convincingly.

"Nonsense, my dear," he replied. "I shall look
forward to it . . . I'll see you at seven."

Then he, too, left and Melanie was all alone.
She went to the guest room, for she suddenly felt
very tired. She knew it was only an emotional let-
down, but she needed very much to lie down and
rest.

As soon as she walked into the room, she saw

the florist's box on the bedside table. Immediately she opened the card.

"Sweet dreams," was all it said . . . with no signature. She looked at the box as if she was trying to read Sterling's mind. Was he genuinely kind? Or was he, like so many other people in her life, putting up a facade? Too early to find out, she thought. And perhaps too late also.

For a minute she stood holding the exquisite golden orchids, admiring their russet tongues and velvety beards. Then she phoned the kitchen.

"Nicholas, I've been told that orchids keep better in the refrigerator."

The mechanical voice came back, "I'll-be-right-there-Mum."

As soon as Nicholas had picked up the box of orchids and asked Melanie how she would prefer her steak at dinner, she slipped out of her clothing and lay on the bed. She made an effort to close her eyes. In her attempt to fall asleep she drifted into an empty dizziness; she had to touch and squeeze the quilt a few times to realize where she was. When the sensation of being lost in a hostile, alien room became too strong, she turned on the light and sat up in bed.

The apartment was silent, too silent to be real. She thought that Sterling had probably put double glazed windows in the bedroom. She didn't like to think about Sterling, because Sterling was just a big puzzle and the last thing she needed was puzzles. Still, his face kept filling her mind. She attempted to put him together in segments: Sterling in the car, Sterling in her sister's apartment, Sterling kissing her before taking off.

"No," she said to herself, "you are wrong. Sterling could never have noticed you, liked you from the beginning. And the kiss was nothing more than a gesture of sympathy for Alexandra's death." A man like him, she thought, is hardly a novice with women. Then that irrational and outspoken inner voice said, "Yes, but how about love?" She liked that—a devil's advocate on her side. She hugged the quilt and turned the light off once again.

She had been asleep for an hour when Nicholas called to let her know that "Mr.-Sterling-usually-dresses-for-dinner-Mum."

That was fine, because where she had planned to go she should be dressed to the nines. Melanie had not brought many clothes with her, but she had brought one lovely dress that she knew was utterly becoming to her. It was a simple Grecian style in a shade that enhanced her own coloring to perfection.

Her shoulder-length hair had a tendency to a gentle natural wave, and the deep brown undertones were accentuated by the golden highlights that had been bleached by the Arizona sun—the same sun that had tanned her skin a shade that was a tone lighter than the shadows in her hair.

Nicholas brought the orchids with an "Excuse-me-for-saying-how-nice-you-look-Mum," and Melanie smiled her gratitude. But as she held up the

stunning corsage, she was disappointed. Somehow it did not look as she had anticipated, something was wrong. "Of course," she said to herself,
"it's just too much!" She promptly separated the
two orchids and pinned one of them on her shoulder.

She went into the room where Dr. Monroe was
waiting with his aperitif. It was a different girl
whom he now observed. It was not just her exter-
nal beauty that had obviously been accented,
there was an internal glow and her stimulating
conversation, her lighthearted quips, showed him
a strong girl . . . one with a sense of purpose
. . . a very different person from the lost thing he
had worried about on the terrace. She had a plan
now.

As they chatted, he did his best to fill her in on
all the questions she asked about Sterling, and he
was enchanted by her candor and quick ability to
know when to stop. She never did quite do what
he feared she might—she did not ask about Sterling's parents. But he hadn't guessed that her curiosity about Sterling was not romantic interest, but
actually her first step in screening for a possible
suspect in her sister's murder.

Then, as he was about to answer one of her
queries, he noticed a large mosquito poised omi-
nously upon the untanned portion of Melanie's
cleavage, which was exposed by the classic styling
of her gown. Due to the position of the insect, the
area upon which it rested, and to Dr. Monroe's

own background of being first a gentleman, then a doctor, he stared in fascination as he tried to decide how to broach the subject tactfully before the subject broached her.

Fortunately the quandary was resolved when Melanie sliced into her rare filet mignon. The heat and scent of it caused the mosquito to abandon Melanie's breast in confusion for the promise of blood on her plate. She saw it and brushed it away. Fortunately Nicholas also had come in from the kitchen at that moment and immediately notified Penelope, who emitted a supersonic signal to the dining room. It was part of her environmental protection system—the presence of flies or any other insect triggered the electronic repellent that drove them away.

The last two mosquitoes, which had been deactivated during their sojourn in the refrigerator, reactivated while Melanie was at dinner, and now evacuated by Penelope's electronic repellent, drifted out into the night and dropped down to Fifth Avenue street level, where one was killed on impact on the windshield of a blue Chevrolet and the other flew into a passing taxi. It landed on the driver's forehead, raised its stinger, and shoved it between two wrinkles.

A few seconds later the cabbie was dead, his cab crashing into the glass front of Yves Saint Laurent's new boutique for men. He was carrying no passengers at the time, and the death of the driver was listed as a probable heart attack.

* * *

Melanie waited until she was sure Nicholas was asleep, then she walked out to the elevator at the far end of the living room and pushed the button. The door slid open with an almost inaudible hiss.

She stepped in and pressed the down button.

The elevator didn't move.

Melanie pressed again . . . and again. Then she looked up and saw Penelope's electronic eye observing her from the corner.

"Aha!" she said. "Big sister is watching!"

Penelope did not respond.

Feeling ridiculous at the prospect of trying to make friends with a computer, Melanie forced a smile and said, "Hi . . . remember me? I'm Sterling's friend, Melanie . . . I want to go down and buy some magazines . . ."

"Melanie Ross not authorized to exit. Magazines will be found in library to the left of the living room," Penelope wrote on the small screen.

In frustration Melanie mumbled, "Stupid computer!"

Penelope responded with "Am not programmed to reply to insults. Good night, Miss Ross."

Melanie closed her eyes, clenched her teeth, and said "Grrrrrrr," then she laughed, gave up, and went to bed.

CHAPTER SEVEN

Sterling had been many places in the world, both
for pleasure and on behalf of Mann Industries, but
he'd never before seen Marrakesh. The closest
he'd been, other than Casablanca, was Tangiers,
and that was far to the north, and Europeanized.
He was staggered by his first impressions as he
rode in a taxi into the city from the airport in the
late afternoon.

First, the majestic backdrop of the High Atlas
mountains, home of the wild Berber tribes, directly behind the city. Then in the distance the
great minaret, over two hundred feet high, dominating the brick-red city. To Sterling it looked like
the Giralda tower in Sevilla, and he said so to the
driver.

"Same guy!" said the driver, a tanned, blondish young man with crinkled amber eyes and a friendly grin. "Same architect. That old boy really got around. This was built in 1195 . . . or anyway, finished about that time. It's called the Koutoubya. Andalusians built it. Beats me how they managed all these projects without Black and Decker."

Sterling chuckled and asked, "I take it you're not a local boy. How do you happen to be here?"

"Aw, a bunch of us came down a few years ago—just knockin' around. My old lady likes it here. We're both from Montreal. Most of the tourists comin' in here are English- or French-speakin' and I can handle that. We both are into leatherwork on the side, and Marrakesh is where it's at. We're doin' okay here."

Sterling nodded as he looked around. They were coming to the great red wall of Marrakesh that surrounds the city, high and thick, zigzagging off in the distance.

"My God, that's an incredible sight!" he exclaimed.

"Yeah, that always gets 'em. That thing's forty or fifty miles, goin' all around the city. Imagine puttin' up a thing like that—no cement mixers, no dump trucks, no cranes, no nothin' but a hell of a lot of manpower . . . often wonder how many were killed off over the years it took to create some of these architectural masterpieces."

Inside the walls they came to a square—a square

that could, and had, held a million people, bounded on three sides by low market stalls, *souks*, and filled with every kind of activity. There were water carriers with goatskin bags over their shoulders, snake charmers, camel drivers, men getting their heads shaved by old women, young women getting their heads shaved by old men, jugglers, acrobats, magicians, hashish peddlers, a man with trained birds, sword swallowers, a woman selling razor blades and condoms, and everywhere carpets for sale. Rabat and Chicaoua and Bini Ouraaine carpets. A man selling his daughter, circles of caftaned Berbers standing around, bearded men who told stories of the olden days, of Hercules and Alexander the Great, illustrating them with paintings on oilcloth that they flipped over as the story of the glories of Islam progressed.

And everywhere food . . . fly-graced food. Strips of meat, parts of dark chicken, pails of couscous, sections of snake, skewers of shish kebab of every kind stuck into watermelons like banderillas in a bull, breads and honeyed baklava of every shape and combination.

"Some of this stuff is pretty good but I'd stay with the hotel food if I were you. If you're gonna be here awhile, just give me a call and I can take you to places that are okay, clean, good food. Here's my card . . . you want the 'guided tour,' any action, give me a buzz."

"Thank you," said Sterling, turning the card to

see the name. "Thanks, Chuck," he repeated as he put the card in his pocket.

They drove down Bab J'did Avenue and into the courtyard of the old Mamounia, a huge apricot-colored structure of great elegance. Sterling paid the driver saying, "I'll keep you in mind, Chuck, I'll probably need you all right."

Inside the grand lobby Sterling walked to the reception desk with the porter behind him carrying the blue suitcase with almost religious respect.

When Sterling removed his sunglasses, the clerk gave him a smile of fake enthusiasm and said, "How nice to have you with us, Mr. Mann."

Sterling was not surprised. His one brown eye, one blue eye had served as a calling card before.

"Nice to be here," he replied. "Is room five twenty-three reserved for me?"

"No, sir. But room five twenty-five is equally beautiful. We thought it would not make any difference."

Sterling assured him that 525 would be all right and signed the register.

After the porter placed his suitcase in the room, collected his tip, and left with deep bows, Sterling looked around the spacious suite. The taste of the decorator was excellent, and Penelope approved of his thought scanning of the palatial room.

"We have a problem here, sweetheart," he said. "This is not Alexandra's room."

Penelope pointed out that there was a connecting door between the two suites.

Sterling held the wrist terminal close to the lock. "Door lock . . . European style . . . doesn't say what make, set flush with door, appears modern."

Penelope asked if the lock was to be opened immediately.

"No," Sterling said. "Find out if anyone is in there."

Penelope emitted an inaudible signal that penetrated the wall, circled the room, measured temperature, air movement, capacity, and carbon dioxide presence.

"No one," assured Penelope, and to be more precise, she added, "No one alive."

Sterling smiled at the shrewd observation, for Penelope was right. She had no way of knowing whether there was a corpse lying on the bed in suite 523. He held the digital watch against the lock, and several clickings and a few seconds later, the door was unlocked.

"*Inshallah*," said Sterling.

"WTK. I'm not programmed for that language," answered Penelope.

Sterling smiled. "My mistake, sweetheart," he said. "That's one language you will have to be programmed for right away. *Inshallah* means 'will of God.'" He pushed the door, but it was bolted from the inside.

"God damn," he muttered.

"*That*, I understand," said Penelope. "It is not nice."

Sterling walked over to the great oval window and opened it. There was a small porch with a table and two chairs. The ledge that connected all the porches on the garden side of the hotel was half the size of Sterling's foot. In between each porch was an eight-foot length of ledge. Seven feet above the ledge there was a metal drain.

With one bound Sterling was on the rail of the porch. He grabbed the drain. Inching his way along the wall, *willing* his lean body into the side of the hotel, he made it to the porch of the other suite. The double glass doors were open.

As Sterling slipped into the room, Penelope transmitted her congratuations. Moving rapidly, he prepared to get what he came for—fingerprints. Not only Alexandra's, but those of any possible visitors she might have had. He took a low-helium laser pen from his pocket. Its wavelength could be adjusted to cut through glass or split a diamond or punch a hole through a steel plate or perform either acupuncture or fingerprint identification.

Sterling adjusted it now for the latter purpose. The laser light had been proven to be the ideal source of correct fingerprint identification, particularly if one had to cope with thousands of them. The old brush and powder technique would have uncovered *all* of the prints in the room; the laser light would illuminate for Penelope only the ones which emitted radiation equal to Alexandra's. As they carefully scanned the dresser, Penelope stopped Sterling at a corner where prints comparable to Alexandra's were picked up.

"Okay," said Sterling. "Good work. Now let's find any visitors."

He quickly put his sunglasses on. Specially treated to absorb laser light, they changed his view of the room completely. Alexandra's fingerprints showed in bright metallic blue, glowing on the side of the dresser. Penelope soon discovered more of the same. Sterling asked her to pick up any prints made at the corresponding time. The task was fairly simple as the body oil would be wearing out with time and the laser frequency could accurately bring out the ones made on the same dates that Alexandra had left hers in the room.

He was scanning an armchair when Penelope stopped him. "Here," she said.

"Photograph them."

It took her a few seconds to complete the job.

"*Inshallah,*" said Sterling with a sigh.

And then he heard the key in the lock and the door was being opened.

Sterling muttered an oath under his breath and dashed to the nearest door. It happened to be the bathroom door, and after he slipped in, he watched through a crack to see who the occupant might be. A fat Germanic businessman came in and picked up a pair of glasses that he'd obviously forgotten.

Just as the man turned to leave the room, the telephone rang. Sterling could overhear the conversation, which was brief, and he was relieved when he heard the man say, "Yes, I'll be down in a minute."

Again the man turned to go, but then, to Sterling's dismay, stopped for an instant and, unzipping his fly, came directly toward the bathroom.

A glance at the bathroom window showed it to be too small, so he stepped into the tub and hid behind the shower curtain, holding his breath.

The man walked in, flipping on the light switch as he came. Soon Sterling heard the flush and the man, zipping up his pants, turned off the light and left.

The instant the door clicked shut, Sterling moved out of the tub. Hearing the scrunch of cars stopping in the hotel driveway, he looked out the bathroom window. There was an official look about the assemblage. Instinctively he pulled down the blind so that he could better observe without being observed. The police? he wondered as he stepped back from the window. Then he noticed the afternoon sun filtered through tiny perforations in the white plastic blind.

Someone had used an ordinary pin to print this message:

ON A NEW CLEAR DAY YOU CAN SEE
FOREVER

Sterling rolled up the blind and strode toward the door. He opened it very slightly and peered out. He could see what appeared to be plain-clothes police converging from both ends of the corridor.

He closed the door, had Penelope lock it, and went out the way he had come. This time the route was more familiar, and in a rush he managed to get back to his suite as the first knock came.

He waited a second, then said, "Who is it?"

An imperious voice ordered, "Open the door, please."

As he complied, he was confronted with a wall of bulky, rugged-looking men, then slowly the cordon parted and a short, stocky man in a beautifully tailored white silk suit walked toward Sterling with his arms outstretched.

"My friend and colleague," he said in Oxfordian English. "Sterling Mannl"

CHAPTER EIGHT

Penelope congratulated Sterling for passing the test once more: Despite the pressure of recent events, the encounter with the Moroccan secret police, and, finally, the surprise of seeing his good friend, Prince Ali Moullah, on his doorstep, Sterling had remained reasonably calm. His temperature, pulse, and respiration ranged between normal and slightly elevated. That Penelope rated as excellent.

Prince Ali Moullah had always been a great practical joker. He reminded Sterling of the time when he, Prince Ali Moullah, had arrived incognito in Paris and Sterling had sent a regiment of majorettes to welcome him in the lobby of the Plaza Athenée! Sterling, in turn, recalled how Ali had reciprocated, sending a string quartet orches-

tra to play by Sterling's bed at the hospital when
he learned that his good American friend had broken a leg skiing.

So, of course, when the "authorities" (carefully
avoiding to specify whether airport police, cus-
toms, or hotel clerk) had informed him of Sterling's arrival, he decided to pay him a direct visit.

"What a magnificent coincidence that you
should arrive on our anniversary!" exclaimed the
Prince.

"For weeks your great admirer, the Princess
Zahra-Maar, has been planning a glorious celebration for this very day. Fireworks, Dom Perignon
for the foreign guests, an orchestra down from Europe, and now you are here to celebrate with us
. . . how happy she will be!"

Sterling had no opportunity to accept or refuse,
for Prince Ali Moullah went on. "A car will come
for you at nine thirty sharp. How wonderful it is
to have you with us for this great occasion, my
friend!"

After Ali Moullah and his entourage had left,
Sterling deactivated Penelope's termini so that he
could put his thoughts in order without interference from a very logical computer. There were
times when human intuition, while very imprecise,
led one to formulate ideas that were beyond the
scope of the conclusions that could be drawn from
programmed information. He knew that he could
lose some of his own memory bank if he did not
exercise it. He needed to examine his own motiva-

tion in these bizarre circumstances into which he had so willingly involved himself.

Alexandra had been a strong, dominating woman. Not really his kind; yet he had found her attractive and interesting when he had come to know her during the interval in which she had conducted her interview with him and the taped report on Mann Industries. Being a warm and compassionate person, his response to her call for help had been natural, and her implied promise of intrigue, mystery, and earthshaking events had aroused his innate curiosity.

Now he had the message, "On a new clear day you can see forever." Could it be anything but, "On a *nuclear* day . . . ?" But what did that mean? Another world war?

Marrakesh was the crossroads of trading information. Could Alexandra have been buying? What information and from whom? Perhaps Penelope would give him some help on that. It was a good break to have been invited to Ali Moullah's party—the important people would all be there, and Sterling would be able to ask questions and detect liars.

He reactivated Penelope, closed his eyes, and requested her to play some nice music and awaken him at eight. Penelope turned on "Meditations" from *Thaïs*.

Prince Ali Moullah's gold-plated Rolls-Royce, chauffered by an elegant Berber in a djellaba, picked Sterling up at nine to drive him to the palace. But just before leaving the room, Sterling took a small vial of blue liquid, put it in a glass of water, and coughed as he drank it.

"That gives you six hours of immunity," said Penelope.

"It tastes terrible!"

"Consider the alternative," she said.

The palace was not far from town toward the spectacular Atlas mountains, which were now platinum-plated by the pale half-moon. Above the pink walls of the palace gardens, a yellow-orange nimbus from the torches and the candlelight glowed, and he could hear the lively music of a European orchestra as it wafted over the parapets.

The great door, studded with twenty shields, swung open. Inside Sterling was greeted by a butler and a maid. He looked around the foyer, done in Scheherazade modern, but with ancient Moorish armor on the walls and crossed lances running up the great staircase, which snaked down from the upper floor.

He was ushered past the marble pillars and through the big glass doors into a fairyland that was the hedged garden. It was as long as a football field, with torches and waiters in livery and jugglers performing, and around the dance platform were table after table of magnificently presented food. Some couples were eating at tables, others dancing, many just milling around. Most, like Sterling, were dressed in white.

A florid-faced Frenchman who was with a
group of young people waved and called out tip-
sily to Sterling. Sterling smiled, waved, and kept
walking. He knew the man, a jet-setter from
Cannes whom he seemed to run into all over the
world. Many attractive women turned to stare at
Sterling as he made his way to his host. The
Prince was, as usual, direct.

"Sterling, old man, seriously, what brings you
to our land?" he asked. "You never were one for
idle travel."

"You're right, Mou. Tell me, does the name Alexandra Robinson mean anything to you?"

The Prince scowled as he thought and finally
said, "No, old boy, I'm sorry," shaking his head.

A glance at the stress analyzer on his wrist told
Sterling that the man was telling the truth.

"Why do you ask?"

"A friend said she had been here at the Mamounia
just before she was murdered."

Prince Ali Moullah shook his head again. Then
he said, "But wait, I can tell you who might
know . . . she's in the business of buying and
selling information and she is here. Her name is
Natasha Kern."

He led Sterling over to a small, stunning black-
haired woman who was standing near the fountain.

Natasha's eyes widened slightly as she shook
hands with Sterling, and she held his hand just a
trifle longer than is usual as she asked, "Have you

only just come to our city?" The accent seemed Russian, although her English was impeccable.

"Today," he replied as he looked into gorgeous but enigmatic eyes. Natasha was very beautiful and about the same age as Alexandra had been. Firm breasts were outlined gently under the crepe de chine that clung to her lovely torso, slender but well formed. As she smiled up at him, her lips were moist and slightly overpainted to make them appear fuller and enhance the whitest of teeth.

"Your name seems familiar. I'm almost positive someone has mentioned it to me before," he said, pausing as if to reflect on this. "It couldn't have been Alexandra Robinson, could it?"

Natasha's thick, naturally dark eyebrows contracted as she replied, "Robinson? I don't think I know the name."

A surreptitious glance at his wrist told him she was lying. She did it well, he thought.

She accepted his invitation to dance, saying, "I thought you'd never ask!" and the heady odor of wild roses engulfed him as she glided into his arms, placing her hand on his shoulder light as eiderdown, and the scent of champagne mixed with the roses.

Sterling and Natasha were dancing their fourth dance under the stars, when the fat Englishman came waddling toward the assistant receptionist at the Mamounia; the concierge was occupied with an arriving guest.

"Key to room five twenty-five, please," he said casually.

"Certainly, sir," said the boy, taking the key from the hook on the rack.

"Good night."

"Night, sir."

The Englishman entered the elevator and pushed a button. As the doors closed and the lift ascended, the man quickly removed the big key-ring, shoved it into his coat pocket, took out an identical-looking ring from his other pocket, and snapped it on. Then he pushed the stop button, followed by the lobby button.

He strode back to the desk, saying, "My good man, bit of an error here. You gave me five twenty-five . . . I'm in two fifty-five."

"Oh, sorry, sir! Name, sir?"

"Houseman, Edward A. Houseman."

The youth looked at his chart. "Right you are, sir. It is Mr. Mann who's in five twenty-five."

Meanwhile Sterling had hoped to get away from the party without attracting attention, but as he was escorting Natasha out of the palace, Prince Ali Moullah saw them and protested, "Sterling, it's bad enough that you should leave so early, but to steal the prettiest girl away from us is really bad form . . . unforgivable!"

"Natasha claims she was too fond of your great champagne and asked me to drive her home. Sorry if I'm beating your time, old boy."

Prince Ali Moullah gave Sterling a dig in the ribs with his elbow and with a satyr's smile said, "I envy you tonight, my friend."

Natasha's maroon Porsche was brought around and Sterling drove back toward the hotel. As she chatted pleasantly about the party and nestled close to him with her hand casually on his thigh, Sterling kept glancing in the rearview mirror. It seemed that a black sedan, out of all the traffic, was always there behind them . . . quite far back, but always there.

Silently he asked Penelope for information. It came back quickly.

"Large sedan stays at three hundred twenty to three hundred fifty feet behind you."

Sterling kept his eyes on the sedan, slowing down gradually.

"Anything wrong?" Natasha asked.

"Not really . . . . just hate to drive fast through these streets," he replied as he checked the mirror.

The black sedan maintained its speed and in a minute or so passed the maroon Porsche and disappeared.

"You thought we were being followed," Natasha declared.

Sterling turned to look at her in surprise. "Followed?" he asked in an innocent voice. "Why?"

"It's not uncommon in Marrakesh," she said sleepily, as she sat back in the bucket seat and closed her eyes with a tiny smile.

As they swung into the hotel courtyard, Sterling stopped the car in front of the main gate. Natasha murmured, "I have a little bungalow at the end of the garden . . . just drive around the corner and into the patio." She hesitated, then added, "Unless you prefer to sleep alone tonight."

Sterling was rather put off by her aggressive bluntness.

He turned to Natasha. "King-size bed?"

"The Shah never complained."

"Ah, but he was a small man."

"Well, 'tis not so big as a barn door, but t'will suffice . . ."

His eyes widened. "You read Shakespeare?"

"I read everything . . . including you, like a book," said Natasha, giving him a sidewise look, her smile slightly challenging.

"That's kind of you, Natasha. A very nice idea. But I am very tired and have work to do."

"Please come," she coaxed winningly. She looked so young and beautiful. "I'll drive on back . . . I'll be waiting for you."

"Maybe tomorrow night," he promised.

He went into the hotel and asked for his key. Penelope was talking to him. She had checked with the CIA memory bank and found out that the fingerprints belonged to Natasha Kern, a Russian defector and ex-KGB agent who had been "sold" to the Shah's Savac after leaving Russia. When the Shah's regime terminated in Iran, she had followed him to Morocco and had stayed on,

establishing a "shop" for buying and selling information.

The clerk handed him his key. Almost at the
same time Penelope flashed to his brain: "Device
emitting subsonic signals."

Sterling looked off in the direction Natasha had
driven, bouncing the key in his hand. He caught
the key decisively, put it into his pants pocket,
walked out into the garden, and started across the
vast moonlit lawn between the rows of orange
trees toward her cottage.

Someone watched Sterling go . . . and smiled
to himself. It was the fat Englishman, who was sitting on the patio in the shadows, just outside the
noisy bar. He was in a tuxedo and beside him was
the little mirrored cage. Making a grunting, chuck-
ling noise, he took the cage on his lap, opened
the door, and started to extract the bat.

Suddenly three Americans came out of the door
from the bar, and the Englishman quickly closed
the door to the cage. The woman was fortyish,
gray-blond, dressed in a low-cut sequinned evening dress, attractive in a Lauren Bacall style. She
had a bottle of champagne in one hand and a glass
in the other. One man, sixty and fat, appeared to
be her husband, the sleek younger man her Italian
lover.

She breathed the night air deeply. "Lord God,
wasn't it stuffy in there . . ."

The young Italian, quite drunk, saw the Englishman in the shadows.

"Speaking of stuffy, sir, you don't look as though you're having much fun . . . have some champagne with us."

The Englishman, watching in frustration as Sterling disappeared, rose, saying, "Thank you."

She was sitting in the big wicker chair with the fan back on the porch, a glass of champagne in her hand. But the look in her eyes was no longer seductive as she said, "So, now we are alone. Shall we talk business?"

Sterling realized she was neither as drunk as he thought nor in an erotic mood. She was just what Penelope had reported: a sophisticated merchant with high selling skills. Sterling raised a questioning eyebrow.

"When you asked me about Alexandra, I knew you were in Marrakesh for information. Am I right?"

"Yes, you are right. I'm here to buy."

"Same story, right?"

"Right."

"How much do you know?"

He sat on the chair next to her. "Enough. But I want to hear it from you. From the top."

She told him everything he expected to hear. And much that he hadn't expected.

Alexandra had come to Marrakesh to buy details on a story about which she already had some basic facts. She couldn't come up with the amount of money Natasha wanted, but they finally made a satisfactory exchange.

"She was a good, how you say, wheeler and dealer," Natasha said, sipping her champagne slowly. "I knew the story was not worth all that much so I came down. Alexandra made some phone calls and we made the deal."

"You ripped her off, in other words. Right?" said Sterling calmly.

Natasha looked at him with a sly smile.

"Stop bluffing, Sterling," she said smoothly. "You've been bluffing all along. You know nothing about the story. But I don't really care. Alexandra paid me for it, you are here to get what she paid for, so I might as well give it to you."

Sterling sat quietly as Natasha related her incredible tale. "The Americans and the Russians are joining forces in a project to develop a new kind of energy, substituting for oil. There is an establishment somewhere in neutral territory where they are conducting experiments on a new, efficient, and inexpensive form of fuel."

"That certainly sounds like a step forward," mused Sterling.

"Of course, and then there would no longer be this dependence upon the OPEC nations."

"That's speculation," Sterling said. "Who would kill to protect speculation?"

Natasha filled her glass once more.

"I've read somewhere, I think it was *Time* magazine, that you have an IQ of one hundred and eighty-five. Don't underestimate mine." She drew closer to him.

"If the Americans and the Russians join forces in a very important project, the security surrounding it would be extremely tight . . . with the CIA and the KGB working together. But could the CIA and the KGB ever really work together . . . ?"

Sterling stared at Natasha attentively.

Natasha continued, "Not likely. So the security would be assigned to a third party, an independent contractor. Do you think whoever got the job would consider what Alexandra was planning to do 'speculation'? By exposing her 'scoop,' I think it's called, this multibillion-dollar project would be ruined. What about the PLO and the Arabs with their grenades and terrorist techniques?"

Sterling was carefully measuring everything she was saying. "Do you know anything more about the kind of energy they're working on?"

Natasha stood up and touched his face with her fingers, which were cold from holding the champagne glass.

"I do know a lot of things," she said gently.

"But you are not afraid for your life? If they killed Alexandra, they might kill you," Sterling suggested.

"Professional hazard," she shrugged. "There's a risk in every job." Then she added as if to herself, "I'm not planning to stay in Marrakesh much longer."

Sterling understood. Merchants of information

found it wiser to keep moving, both from the standpoint of procuring material and presenting a moving target.

Sterling then decided to divulge his information in the hope of getting more from Natasha. He said, "I found a message in Alexandra's room—'on a new clear day you can see forever'—what could she have meant by that?"

She smiled playfully and sat on his lap like a little girl. "Good at riddles?" she asked.

"I got the 'nuclear day' part . . . what about the rest?"

"I'm afraid that's a twenty-five-thousand-dollar question, my friend."

"Well, I suppose that's better than sixty-four thousand . . . I'll have to go to my room to get my checkbook."

"Don't worry, I've checked your D and B, as you Americans say. You can pay me in the morning."

Sterling took it to mean she would also tell him in the morning, and so he did not push the issue, having sensed her mood had changed.

He apologized for the cliché when he asked, "Really, what's a nice girl like you doing in a job like this?"

"It's a good life," she replied. "When you have lived in the Soviet Union as I have, you learn to appreciate independence."

"You know . . . you've heard . . . what happens to people who trade in information?"

She came forward and leaned over him, her

breasts almost brushing his face, and the scent of wild roses engulfed him in a warm feeling. "I'm a big girl, you know," she said conspiratorially. "And, so far, I'm doing very well . . . very, very well . . ." Then with a little crooked smile she added, "In business, that is."

Taking him by the hand and walking toward the bedroom, she said, "I do have talent in other areas."

The moonlight was spreading shades of silvery blue over the dark room, and as Natasha removed her nightgown and turned back the pink silk sheets, she said, "But you are right, Sterling. I really *am* a nice girl. I come from a very important family . . ."

As she spoke, she carefully draped her nightgown on a chair next to the bed.

Sterling watched her, then pointed to the nightgown and smiled. "In case of fire?"

She gave a low, throaty laugh. "In case of fire."

He was asleep in Natasha's arms when he sensed it. He did not hear it, and since the alien presence was not in the room, Penelope gave no warning. But the extraordinary sensitivity he had been born with warned him that there was something hostile moving about in the garden near the cottage.

He slipped out of bed silently and pulled on the pair of pants on the chair near the bed. He went out the double doors that opened onto the garden, making sure that his bare feet made no sound on the tiles. The moment he stepped out onto the lawn, he saw a shadow move behind the hedge. He started for it, saw it slip out from behind the hedge to the row of orange trees. Even with the moonlight and his exceptional eyesight, Sterling could only guess that it was a large man dressed in some flowing Moorish garment. Now he disappeared altogether, and soon Sterling found himself at the far end of the garden with no sign of the quarry.

Meanwhile, Natasha was awakened by a sound—the slap of sandals on the patio tiles. She raised her head and a faint silhouette was framed in the doorway.

"Sterling," she said drowsily, holding out her arms, "what are you doing prowling about? Come back to bed, darling."

But it wasn't Sterling, and she knew it the moment she saw the bright bluish light, a sudden reflection of the moonlight, on a Moroccan dagger. She had no chance to scream as the pink silk sheets on the bed turned crimson.

The fat Englishman's eyes were well accustomed to the night after his long vigil on the porch, and when he saw Sterling at the end of the garden, he opened the door to the little cage. Tenderly, he took out the bat, removed the muzzle from its head like a falconer taking off the hood of his favorite hawk, and stroked it once before launching it into the night.

The bat zigzagged only once around the garden before hovering over Sterling. Then, guided by the keyring in Sterling's pocket, it folded its wings and plummeted down, alighting for a fraction of a second on the man's shoulder, then biting him on the neck.

As it flapped off into the night, Sterling put his hand to his neck, then saw the blood on his fingers.

"How stupid, I forgot the damned key was still in those pants," he thought to himself. He looked around quickly for his enemy, but he could see no one and there was no time to look further. The antidote he had taken so much earlier would have worn off by now. He had to get back to the cottage and to his other jacket quickly.

Curare was a fast poison, he knew, and it worked much more quickly if one moved fast. He forced himself to walk calmly toward the cottage. By the time he was twenty feet from the door, he was staggering and dizzy. He lurched onto the porch and fell to his knees. Gasping, he pulled himself into the sitting room, across the tiles to the chair where he had hung his jacket earlier. When he got there, with one Herculean effort he hauled his upper body up to the seat and groped in the breast pocket of his jacket for the vial. He pulled out the cork with his teeth, drank the blue liquid, and collapsed, knowing that he had taken too much of the antidote, which was almost as strong as the poison itself.

When he awoke hours later, he found himself looking into a great black mustache surrounded by a uniform.

"He is coming around!" announced the mustache.

Sterling narrowed his eyes in an effort to focus. Other mustaches and uniforms were coming at him. It was bright daylight and he could hear the wail of police sirens screaming beyond the garden's walls.

"The assassin awakes," said a rough voice, which seemed somehow connected with the mustache, although the movement of the lips and the sound of the voice seemed to be out of synch.

Sterling looked beyond the bulk of the captain of police and saw the reason for all of this: Natasha's head and both arms were flung over the side of the bed. There was no blood on the white skin of her beautiful face and shoulders, but both breasts were scarlet-encrusted where blood had run down and dripped from the nipples onto the tile floor.

The first-class seat on the Pan Am jet felt comfortable, and Sterling stretched back, shaking off the memories of the past few hours. If it hadn't been for Prince Ali Moullah, he would have been in terrible trouble with the inflexible Moroccan police and the stubborn secret service major who insisted upon "questioning" him in the traditional, one might say rather severe, Arabian way.

The Prince angrily ordered him released over

the phone. "How *dare* you accuse a friend of ours, this great inventor, benefactor of mankind, of such a foul deed!" and then personally came to the hotel to see that his friend was all right. Ali Moullah had said how sorry he was that this had happened to Sterling. He apologized for failing to warn Sterling as he left the party that Natasha's occupation and past connections did not make her the safest girl to squire home, even though she was by far the most beautiful.

"Whoever killed Natasha was probably hired by the Iranian radicals who want everyone connected with the Shah dead," the Prince explained. "It is most upsetting to me that my country, which is peaceful and in no way involved with such dealings, should be subjected to this sort of thing."

Ali Moullah then escorted Sterling to the airport and six plainclothes policemen accompanied him to the plane, which was under tight security. After saying a heartfelt good-bye to the Prince, he dropped into his seat.

After the chilling experiences of the past night, he felt completely drained. A normal human being might well have died—either from the curare or from the overdose of antidote. His body was still weak, and he felt grateful for the warmth and the security of the plane and the solicitous care of the attendants.

Now he was almost sure about the events that had ended with an attempted double murder: The killer had deliberately made the noise that had lured him into the garden to be eliminated by the bat while the assassin took care of Natasha. This way it could be made to appear that he, Sterling, had killed Natasha and died of a heart attack while leaving the scene. It fit the pattern established with Alexandra's death. It was apparent that they did not want to risk failure in a confrontation with him.

But, poor Natasha . . . such a beautiful, fascinating woman. She'd led a very precarious life . . . it seemed somehow doomed to end in disaster.

If what Natasha had disclosed to Sterling was true, then someone, somehow, would be trying to sabotage the Russian-American project, turning it into a nuclear holocaust. That was obvious since the project was a peaceful one, aimed only at the development of a new nondestructive form of energy. With Natasha dead, the riddle of the window blind in Alexandra's bathroom was still unsolved.

As soon as he was home and safe, he would have to feed this information to Penelope. In the meantime, he had made a few simple but important moves. He had asked Dr. Monroe, via Penelope, to take Melanie from the New York penthouse to the summer cottage in Connecticut. Mann Industries had been instructed to ship the ESV to the summer cottage in a sealed container. Sterling was not yet sure whether there was one conspiracy or two, and whether the target was not his revolutionary flying car as well as himself.

Penelope's information buzzed in his ear: "Your vital signs are showing elevation. Suggest you get some sleep. I will watch over you . . . trust me."

Now, as he was about to drift off to a much-needed sleep, he thought of Melanie. For some strange reason, the well-educated, well-traveled, wealthy, adventurous playboy image that Sterling presented to the world masked a vulnerability that was responding to the special chemistry of wit, courage, and warmth that Melanie possessed.

Sterling smiled and relaxed.

CHAPTER NINE

In Old Mitford, Connecticut, at an isolated facility, an unmarked, plain gray security van pulled up in front of a building in the dark. An insignia of an atom truncated by a bolt of lightning was barely visible over the front door. Behind the building the background was obscured by a disc that looked like a huge radar saucer. Two men in plainclothes got out of the van and walked quickly into the building. An armed guard stopped them.

"We're come for Serial Number seventy-eight-eleven," said one of them.

"Got the papers?" growled the guard in a bored voice.

The orders were produced; the guard made a quick phone call to verify them. Then he walked

over to a panel and pressed a button which unlocked the door behind him.

"Okay, seventy-eight-eleven," the guard mumbled.

A chimpanzee came out, cautiously looking
around.

The men laughed. "That's Serial seventy-eight-
eleven?" said one. "I thought we were picking up
an astronaut!"

"Don't laugh," said the guard, glaring at the
speaker. "This monk's been in space twice. He's
classified 'Cosmic' in NASA files and is probably a
hell of a lot smarter than you."

"If you say so," said one of the men as he
started to reach out for the chimpanzee's hand.
"He doesn't bite, does he? That's all we care
about."

The men escorted the animal out of the building, put him in the back of the van, and locked the
door. The chimp made unhappy noises in the dark
van; he was used to riding in front. But the men
ignored him as they drove away.

Several minutes later, as they were driving
through the small town that led to the freeway approach, the primate bent down and examined the
locking device on the door. It was not a complicated mechanism, and by inserting a splinter he
found on the floorboard, he manipulated the
latch. Chimpanzees even in the wild customarily
use sticks to extract insects from holes, and this
chimp had lost none of his original instincts. He

peered out and knew he was traveling too fast to make a jump. Then the vehicle slowed and stopped, for there was a traffic light flashing red at the intersection. Just as the ape was about to jump, another car slowed up behind the van. The chimpanzee leaped nimbly to the hood of the car, and as the startled motorist watched, the animal neatly closed the doors of the van so the banging doors would not alert the guards, then scampered off the car and disappeared into the quiet of the sleeping village. The driver then honked his horn to attract the attention of the driver of the van.

"Impatient bastard," muttered the guard as he gunned ahead.

Then, just as the man behind the van was about to come alongside to indicate that they had lost their cargo, the van reached the freeway approach and zoomed away. Having made his effort to do the right thing and failed, the driver, who was a local resident, shrugged and went home.

The long flight from Lisbon ended at New York's wet and windy Kennedy Airport. Sterling flew his helicopter to the summer cottage in Connecticut, where a calm and smiling Dr. Monroe was enjoying Melanie's rage. The depression and sadness of Alexandra's death and the strain of the funeral was slowly turning into anger, as she felt a prisoner there, unable to help, kept totally in the dark.

"Well," Sterling asked, "are you furious or just brooding?"

"Just brooding at present, but don't push your luck," she snapped.

Dr. Monroe gave Sterling a meaningful look, shook his head, and said in a low voice, "Cabin fever. She's been this way ever since you called with instructions to leave the penthouse. What are you going to do?"

"I'm going to fix us some dinner," Sterling said with a grin. "Melanie, would you like to join us?"

Melanie shook her head and looked stubbornly out the window.

Mixing the eggs and grated cheese and heating the pan with fresh butter, Sterling told Dr. Monroe about his experience in Marrakesh and the giant puzzle of the new clear day. By the time the omelet was golden-brown, Sterling had included all the essentials.

"Uncle Hank, will you fly to Washington tomorrow? I think it's time I met the President," Sterling said.

Dr. Monroe agreed, then went to bring Melanie to the table. Reluctantly she came.

Looking at the fluffy omelet, she said, "I'd rather expected the traditional bread and water."

Sterling filled her glass with red wine and told her everything about Marrakesh. She seemed very interested in Nastasha, so Sterling decided to delete a few unimportant details. Although Melanie's questions were carefully phrased, he detected some thinly veiled jealousy, so he skipped a few key scenes. Melanie watched him speak, and the more she studied his face, the more convinced she was that Sterling was telling her the truth but, somehow, not the whole truth.

After dinner Dr. Monroe and Sterling excused themselves as together they got the doctor packed to go to Washington, discussing various details as they worked.

When Dr. Monroe said his good-byes and left, Melanie said, "Well, you got him out of the way, so what's next? With all this secrecy, how do I know that *you* didn't kill Alexandra?"

Sterling looked at her quizzically and said, "I see your point. Please sit down and I'll try to tell you everything I've learned so far, but you'll have to believe me when I say it's all very sketchy."

He poured a cognac for her and said, "I do not understand why you are so hostile toward me. I like you."

"Oh, bull," she said. "You just need me for some purpose." And she thought, Why *am* I so damned bitchy; he really hasn't been anything but nice to me? as she watched him over the rim of the snifter. He was looking better with every sip she took . . . Uh-oh, she thought, and said to Sterling, "Can't we have some music or something? The noises in this creepy old house bug me."

Sterling got up and put a stack of records on the record player, asking her preferences.

"Oh, anything with a good beat to it . . . I love to dance," she replied.

"So do I," Sterling said, and started to roll back the Aubusson.

Melanie hopped up off the sofa and came toward him in time to the music, and they admired each other's movements as they gave their repertoire of stylish steps. The old stereo plopped and hissed and suddenly a lovely Neil Diamond song began and Sterling took Melanie in his arms.

"Why would anyone with all the far-out electronic equipment you have still use an old turntable?" she asked.

"Belongs to Doctor Monroe," he answered, wondering what kind of "vital signs" Penelope was recording as he held this girl close.

"Naturally, you *would* have to be the world's best dancer," she murmured to the pocket of his jacket as she put her head on his chest. His hard body was pressed against hers, and she felt good and warm and sensual as he moved so smoothly to the music, guiding her expertly with just the subtlest of pressures, his hand on her back. God, she thought, why does he have to be so damned attractive?

Finally the record player shut off, but Sterling and Melanie were not aware of the silence. Suddenly Penelope came out with: "Shall I . . . take over now and play more music for you?"

There was a moment of awkwardness as Sterling collected himself. Then he said, "Come, it's getting late . . . I'll show you to your room."

Melanie looked up at him like a little pixie and

said, "What about *your* room?" Then she reached
up and kissed him. He kissed her hard in return
and then again and again, feeling her good body
tight against him, his hands traveling over her
breasts, his gentle fingers feeling her nipples bur-
geon.

Poor Penelope was simply not programmed for
what was to follow. A sense of delicacy caused
Sterling to remove his computer-watch and put it
on the dresser, totally deactivated to ensure his
privacy. Though his hearing would not be perfect,
the quiet beauty of the moment gave Sterling a
marvelous sensation of relaxation.

Nonetheless, he had to be cautious. As Melanie
watched in fascination, he quietly set up his auxiliary alarm system. As he strung fine wire from the
bedsheets to the several plants outside the door
that led to the enclosed patio garden off the bedroom, he explained to her that it was a known fact
that plants were hypersensitive and quite respon-
sive to danger or violence of any sort. He told her,
"If anyone should try to get in here while we're
asleep, they'll set off an electrical current, low
voltage, but enough to wake us. If they come
within six feet of any of the plants out there, I'll
know it."

She helped him string the wire, and as they finished the project, he looked up at her. Her serious
sweet face caused him to lose his train of thought
and he went toward her.

She was saying something . . . he could hear

her voice but couldn't understand the words. But he could read her eyes, read her lips, and as he closed his arms around her lovely little body, he could feel her heart beating . . . all of his senses were intensified, including a sixth sense that told him this girl was no phony, and the emotions he was experiencing were new to him. Sterling was in love.

It was sometime past midnight when a wiry, dark figure appeared on top of the eight-foot wall of the garden outside the bedroom where Melanie and Sterling were sleeping so contentedly. As silent as a shadow, he dropped to the sun deck, looked around slowly in the pale moonlight, and then moved stealthily toward the bedroom door. As he drew closer, he came within a yard of a philodendron plant. Immediately the wired plant sensed the alien presence and reacted.

At the first faint sensation, the electrical shock, although very mild, snapped Sterling awake. Seeing the dark, crouched shape silhouetted in the doorway, he grabbed the gun from the night table. Simultaneously he drew his knees up, planted his feet against Melanie's hip, and shoved her off the bed. He flipped himself off his side of the bed as he fired once at the invader.

The figure gave more of a surprised gasp than a groan as it sagged to the ground.

Sterling snapped the bedside light on, slipped Penelope's termini around his wrist, and holding the pistol at ready, he ran over to examine his victim.

"Good Lord!" he said as he looked down.

"Congratulations." Melanie looked at the chimpanzee with disbelief. "You've just killed a poor monkey."

She untangled her naked body from the bedsheets and came over to them.

"A chimpanzee," he corrected. "And he isn't dead, this gun just zaps . . . get a towel . . . I'll get some ice."

When Sterling came back from the kitchen with a bowl of ice, Melanie was kneeling beside the chimp, who was already sitting up as she applied the damp cloth to its forehead. The chimp's eyes were still glazed, but one huge hand weakly stroked Melanie's arm as though in gratitude.

"Look, Sterling . . . he has a collar," she said. "He's somebody's pet!"

Sterling knelt and looked at the tag that dangled at the chimpanzee's throat. There were vertical black markings on it like the identification-price codes on supermarket goods for fast checking at the counter.

"If he's somebody's pet, they don't seem to want him back in a hurry with this kind of tag," said Sterling. "He's some kind of experimental animal."

After a few minutes the chimp was revived enough to get to his feet. Melanie and Sterling each took a hand and walked him into the bathroom. The chimp pulled a bath towel off the rack, sat down in a corner, and pulled the towel over his head.

"Let him sleep it off," said Sterling. "We'll make inquiries in the morning." He gently pulled Melanie to him. "Meanwhile . . . ?" he asked.

Her firm breast felt good against his chest, and her body squirmed against him as she softly replied, "Meanwhile!"

He walked her backward toward the bed. They laughed as she toppled onto it with him landing on top of her, and they heard a soft echoing sound of approval from the bathroom. The chimpanzee seemed to recognize the sounds of lovemaking as the normal jungle mating noise of one of the greater apes.

"Possums eat moonbeams," Sterling thought he heard as his eyes came open, and he knew he was not dreaming.

"Dewy, dewy fish come frog."

Sterling sat up in bed and shook his head. The morning sun was streaming in through the French doors. Was he hallucinating? It sounded like Nicholas's voice but a demented Nicholas, and anyway Nicholas was back at the penthouse. Sterling's hearing was usable but not perfectly normal. After his surgery his audiograms showed good reception and discrimination in the lower frequencies but a dramatic drop in the higher register. Therefore, when he modified the speaking device for Nicholas, he adjusted the tone to come through at his most sensitive frequency. Thus with Penelope disconnected, the voice of Nicholas could prove to be useful as a backup system. But what was Nicholas doing here?

Sterling looked around. Melanie was not in sight. He went into the bathroom. The chimp was gone. As he wrapped a towel around him and started for the living room, he heard the computer voice again.

"Birds and ketchup soup."

Melanie looked up as he approached. "Oh, Sterling!" she exclaimed. "This is such a marvelous device. Imagine how wonderful it will be for my students if even an animal can use it!"

The chimpanzee was holding the small talking device such as Nicholas used. The ape, its attention totally focused on the computer, was poking the buttons, taking time with each one as though every word were of cosmic importance.

"Butterfly . . . music . . ." said the weird, artificial voice. "Asphalt."

Sterling and Melanie laughed delightedly as the ape continued his performance. He, too, was delighted with the attention he was getting.

Melanie stood up and said, "Coffee is ready and I'll be back in a moment to fix your eggs."

Sterling did not respond but sat with the chimp, fascinated by the animal's intelligence.

Melanie returned from the bedroom wearing a fresh-looking cotton dress and flaunting her left arm with mock pride—on her wrist was the computer terminal.

"I think Penelope looks divine on me—"

Sterling grabbed her arm and ripped the watch off her wrist. "Don't you ever do that again!"

"You mean," she retorted hotly, "it's your toy and no one else is allowed to play with it!"

He turned the "watch" over. Melanie saw two thin needles, no longer than an eighth of an inch, suddenly spring out like fangs of a cobra.

"You were seconds away from receiving twenty thousand volts—instant paralysis," he explained. "Penelope is programmed to read my temperature, pulse, and skin tissue. Only mine. If anyone else puts her on, she knows it. She waits only twenty seconds."

Sterling watched the thin needles retract automatically. He put the computer terminal on.

Silent and shaken, they went into the kitchen. Melanie poured their coffee and sat down. They did not look at each other for several minutes, then Melanie finally said, "All right, give it to me straight. No joke, you really are a spy?"

Sterling grinned. "I thought you'd never ask."

Melanie shook her head. "Who's going to believe my story of 'what I did on my vacation'? I mean, how am I going to explain flying over the Grand Canyon in an automobile and plants that set off alarms and computers that can kill you . . . who'll believe any of this?"

"Your sister would, if she were still alive. She

had a pretty good idea of what Mann Industries was all about," Sterling mused.

"I'm sorry," said Melanie. "I'm just upset . . . it isn't just having all these sudden nodding acquaintances with the 'grim reaper.' The truth is, I haven't even gone to bed with a man in a long time . . . puts a strain on a girl's emotional equilibrium . . . this sort of thing."

Sterling gave her a reassuring smile, then he asked, "Have you heard of industrial espionage?"

"I don't know anything about any kind of espionage except things like James Bond," she admitted.

"Well, it's not far from those James Bond tales. When you have important inventions at stake, a lot of other people's money involved, you have to be careful."

"Tell me more," she said. "I loved *Star Wars*."

He tried to explain to her that a lot of people would kill for the blueprints to the ESV or access to Penelope's design.

"I suppose that microwave oven on the front of the car was designed for Julia Child, right?"

He admitted that the device was a weapon and that the Pentagon had a lot to do with the ESV's development.

Melanie looked out of the window and shook her head, thinking, nice going, Melanie. You do your Jane Fonda act for years and then get yourself screwed by a pawn of the Pentagon who builds cars that turn people into French fries . . .

She finished her coffee and stood up.

"If I walk out of here, they will probably get me before I have a chance to go to the police. If I stay here, I'll probably be killed by one of your toys. I don't like the choice . . . God, what I wouldn't give to be back in the world of normal human beings."

"Sex makes for sunny days," came the electronic voice from the living room.

Sterling and Melanie looked at each other, then both of them laughed. The tension was released. They went into the living room to see what their simian friend was up to.

"Where do you suppose he came from?" Melanie asked. "A circus?"

"Not with this collar," said Sterling. "Look here. Aside from the computer identification, there's this . . ." He knelt down and pulled forward a metal tag for Melanie to see. It was an insignia— an atom traversed by a bolt of lightning.

"You know," said Melanie, "I read in a *National Geographic* that a gorilla was taught sign language—some three-hundred signs or more. Not only that, he even taught it to other apes. I wonder if . . ."

She made a simple motion with her hands in front of the chimp's face.

Immediately the chimpanzee dropped his "toy" and focused his attention on Melanie. She repeated the sign for: "Do you understand sign language?"

This time the chimp made the sign for "Yes

Sterling quickly made the signs for: "What are you called?" and the chimp answered: "Number 78—"

"He should have a name," said Melanie.

"Let's give him a good name," said Sterling as he thought, then he smiled. "I always loved the Tarzan books when I was a boy. How about Tarzan's real name, Lord Greystoke?"

Then Sterling and Melanie continued to "talk" with the ape at length. In a primitive way, the animal was able to tell them about his trips into outer space and about his escape.

"This is a very valuable animal," said Sterling. "We have to try to return him. But where? Is he a NASA experiment?" Sterling knew of no installation in the surrounding area.

Then Sterling made the signs for: "Can you guide us to where you came from?"

And the chimp made the sign for "Yes."

Half an hour later they were driving the ESV through a remote wooded area. The chimpanzee, in the front seat between Sterling and Melanie, made cooing sounds of contentment and happiness as he pointed to this or that road; he was clearly elated at being in a position to instruct others what to do rather than the other way around.

When the chimp pointed to a dirt road off to the right that had a sign saying Road Closed, Sterling began to wonder if he might have misinterpreted the animal's signs or perhaps overestimated its intelligence. Yet the creature kept pointing and became quite agitated when Sterling hesitated. They bounced down the road for several miles; then suddenly, they came out into a clearing in the trees. There was a cement complex with a strange giant saucer behind it. They drove up to the door, and Sterling realized that he hadn't overestimated the chimp. Over the entrance was the same logo as that on the animal's collar—an atom traversed by a bolt of lightning.

When Sterling got out of the car, the chimp jumped up and down on the seat and refused to leave.

"This is your home," Sterling signed.

The chimpanzee shook his head violently.

Melanie's attitude with Greystoke was completely different than with Sterling. She treated the chimp much the same as her retarded students—she was the patient teacher, the sympathetic mother.

"Greystoke, are you not happy here?" she spelled out with her fingers.

The chimp shook his head mournfully and tried to cling to Melanie. "Bad place, bad men," he signed.

Sterling pulled the reluctant animal out of the car, and with Melanie holding the other hand, they walked up to the building.

"Do we really have to take him back to where he doesn't want to go?" she asked.

"We can't just up and steal him," Sterling reasoned.

The door opened automatically . . . and slammed shut behind them. Three men faced them, uniformed and with drawn pistols.

"Hello," said Sterling. "We have a reservation for lunch." They did not return his smile.

One of the guards, without lowering his gun, spoke into a small microphone in his hand: "Base, Serial Number 78-11 has been returned . . . with two unclassified."

"Bring the man to me," said a voice. "The other two keep in R-ten for now."

"Yes, sir."

A steel door opened, revealing a windowless room. Sterling could see wheels, knobs, switches, and closed-circuit monitors. Two of the guards grabbed Melanie and the chimpanzee.

"Take your goddamn hands off me," Melanie commanded and drove an elbow into one man's gut.

"Hey, hold it!" protested Sterling, starting to move after them, but the third guard held his pistol pointed at Sterling's chest. With his low forehead and huge shoulders, he looked more simian than Greystoke.

"You're coming with me," he said as the door closed behind Melanie, Greystoke, and their captors. "Keep your hands up."

The man pressed a button and a third door slid open, this time to the outside, to the back of the complex. Sterling saw the gigantic radarlike disc, three-hundred feet across, which looked like some Brobdingnagian saucer. Even as the guard prodded him in the back with the pistol, forcing him to some unknown and probably dangerous destination, the scientist in Sterling marveled at the construction and wondered about its purpose. He stopped to study it. The guard jabbed him in the spine.

"Keep moving, buddy," he growled.

"Please don't do that again," said Sterling quietly. "For your own good."

When the man jabbed him again, Sterling suddenly whirled with the speed of a panther. He caught the hand holding the pistol in his right fist, held the man by his jacket at the throat with his left, and then as the man screamed, he slowly tightened his grip until the fingers clutching the pistol broke with a terrible smashing sound.

The gun fired twice, harmlessly.

Sterling then picked the big man up and flung him against the building as though he were a bag of laundry.

The shot brought six uniformed men out of the other building, all of them with drawn pistols.

Sterling turned to run back to the entrance building where Melanie was, but the steel door had already slid shut. There was only one way to go. Up. Up the side of the great saucer. He easily outran his pursuers to the structure, which looked somewhat like a bull-fighting area with its naked girders around the bowl of the radar-type disc. He leaped up and grabbed the first girder, pulled himself up, and kept climbing as his pursuers clumsily tried to follow him.

As he hauled himself over the rim, he looked down. It was awesome. A great white colosseum, seventy feet deep and three hundred feet across. What in God's name was a radar of this magnitude used for? But this was no time for speculation; below him came the guards. A huge cable was stretched across the saucer; the steel strand was at least a foot and a half wide. He could see trees on the hill on the other side—get across this giant saucer, climb down, circle around, and call for help.

He stepped out on the cable. There was no give, it was not like tight rope walking. Easily he ran out over the span.

"Hold it!" yelled one of the guards, as he stepped out onto the cable and awkwardly tried to follow Sterling. The other five men followed. Sterling was halfway across when the first bullet came. It passed so close to his head that he ducked instinctively. As he did, his foot slipped and he fell.

He fell and he fell. And then he was falling slower, more smoothly. It was like a childhood dream, when one jumped down into the clouds, the wonderfully soft clouds.

"Am I dead?" he asked himself as he floated. "Is this what death is like?"

And yet the scientist in him said, "You are not dead, you are in some weird science-fiction contraption where gravity is canceled out."

That's what this radarlike thing was! A colossal gravity beam projector! Instead of being killed, he was suspended in space, weightless in space like an astronaut!

But coming toward him, "swimming" through the air like a team of sky divers, were six armed and dangerous men. Sterling immediately began "swimming" himself, and having been the anchor man in Yale's finest relay team, he swam better than the guards. But suddenly there was a difference—one of the men opened fire. And then the others did. The only reason the first shots did not hit him was because the weightlessness of the bullets prevented them from going far in the zero gravity. It was a question of time, and Sterling knew it as he twisted and writhed and clawed the air toward the opposite rim of the bowl.

Watching helplessly on the TV monitors was Melanie, locked in the control room with Greystoke. At the sound of the pistol shots, one guard had run out . . . but not before locking her, the chimp, and the other guard in.

The guard that remained with them alternately watched the action on the monitor and Melanie, ignoring Greystoke. Melanie managed to signal to Greystoke as the guard watched the monitor. The ape's eyes brightened as he understood what he was supposed to do. He moved silently behind the seated guard. He clenched his great hands together, raised them over his head, and glanced over at Melanie for approval. She gave a slight nod, and Greystoke brought them down with all his might on the man's cranium. The guard toppled off the chair without a sound.

"Greystoke, winner and new champion!" said Melanie, and the chimp clapped his hands together delightedly for his mission accomplished.

But now Melanie and Greystoke clung to each other as they watched Sterling on the TV monitor. She knew that, in spite of their weightlessness, they could not continue to miss their target for long.

"Oh, Lord, Sterling, look out on the right . . . a guy's gaining on you!" she agonized.

The chimp was screaming as he watched, then he suddenly tugged at Melanie's arm and pointed to the panel, jumping up and down in his excitement.

"What is it Greystoke? What do you want me to do?"

Then she realized that the animal was pointing to the thermo-electric switches next to the TV monitor. Underneath was a brass plate that read Gravity Zero. Off. On. It was switched to On. She waited until she saw Sterling grab the metal rim and pull himself up onto it. Then she spun the wheel to the Off position. The six men stopped "swimming" through the air. They hung suspended grotesquely for a mini-second, then fell sixty feet to their death.

Panting, Sterling looked down at them, relieved but nauseated and wondering the why of it all. Spent and exhausted, he climbed back down the girders from the disc and made his way to the control room. A guard suddenly came around the corner with his gun drawn. Sterling stunned him with one slashing blow to the temple. He found the red button and the door slid open to the control room. Melanie and Greystoke rushed out. Another lever opened the main door and they ran to the ESV.

"Buckle up," he commanded as he threw the gear shift into first, and the automobile's front wheels virtually left the ground as it leaped forward.

They heard the warning sirens behind them. He watched the garage door spring open, saw the powerful cars and Jeeps and men seeming to come from everywhere in pursuit.

As they sped around the corner up into the wooded hill, there were nine cars following them.

Sterling jounced and bounced the ESV back over the "closed road" that had led them into the complex. The rough, wooded terrain made it impossible for him to get maximum speed from the ESV. At last they reached the road from which they had originally turned off and Sterling said to

Melanie, "They assume that we'll head down, back into the village . . . so we'll head up."

As they squealed off the dirt road onto the pavement, Sterling checked the rear TV and saw one car, a brown Chevrolet, about a hundred yards behind them. Then as his eyes went back to the road in front of him, he saw a huge truck parked in front of a house just ahead. The Purest Water This Side of Heaven the sign on the tailgate said, and it was loaded with fifty five-gallon bottles of water laid horizontally in their niches with their necks sticking out. Sterling could see the driver going into a house with a bottle on his shoulder. He swerved the ESV, the left wheels jolting up on the curb, and just managed to skim past the truck and its cargo.

The driver of the Chevrolet tried to emulate Sterling's maneuver, but he didn't spin the steering wheel quite in time. The side of his car scraped the length of the truck and then spun out of control. In his TV mirror Sterling could see the car lurched over on its side, on fire and with the water gurgling out of a dozen truncated bottles whose necks had been abruptly clipped off.

He had a head start now, but before he rounded the next curve he saw the other pursuing cars bypassing the truck and coming up rapidly.

On a straight highway no car in the world could have caught the ESV, but on this winding, wooded road he could not go much faster than they. In two miles they had almost caught up with him; Sterling could see the green Volvo in the lead with two men in it . . . coming . . . coming . . . coming. The road was becoming very steep now, with the mountain on the left and a sheer drop to a ravine on the right. Half a mile later the pursuers were directly behind Sterling . . . he heard the crack of a pistol shot and then another.

Greystoke, who had been enjoying the wild ride, now chattered with fear and put his fingers over his eyes and ears.

Up ahead Sterling saw an ess curve which ended in an abrupt hairpin over a gorge. Quickly he pulled the lever that extended the stabilizer flaps on either side of the car. He pressed the button that fastened the automatic metal straps over them and gunned the car through the ess curve, tires screaming. Then instead of making the sharp turn at the end of it, he went straight ahead, hurtling his car into the air. Sterling flipped two switches. The ESV dipped and fell five feet before the jets took hold and propelled it into crooked flight. Sterling pulled back on the wheel to get its nose up. It pitched and yawed twice . . . then straightened itself.

"Good girl," he muttered.

The pursuers in the Volvo were following so closely that they had no time to correct, and by the time they realized that there was no road where the ESV had gone, they had shot into space and were falling into the ravine below.

* * *

It wasn't more than twenty minutes after the ESV landed on the beach when Melanie emerged from the bedroom carrying her weather-beaten pale blue Samsonite with some difficulty.

Sterling looked at her in surprise, then asked, "Is something wrong?"

"I'm just getting out of here," Melanie snapped.

"I see. Are you furious or just being moody?" he asked with a smile.

"Furious."

"But why, may I ask?"

Melanie continued to half carry, half drag the suitcase across the room. She said in a very quiet and patient tone, as if trying to communicate with one of her handicapped students, "It is probably no fault of yours, but since I've been in your presence, I've seen more violence than in all of my life up to the day we met. I simply can't tolerate it."

"I realize your experiences with me have been horrendous, but I assure you that I have no taste for violence either," Sterling said.

"But you seem to live constantly in the eye of the storm. Perhaps Alexandra did too, but that's why our lives were so different . . . I'm simply not cut out for all of this."

Sterling quietly observed, "I suppose it was Greystoke's idea to KO the guard and cut the power that wasted all those men back on the saucer."

"That's what makes me furious," said Melanie.

"Furious at myself! I'm supposed to be a damned pacifist—a bleeding heart—and now I'm just as bad as you are for God's sake!"

"I see," Sterling nodded. "And where are you going?"

"Anywhere but here."

"And I suppose you're going to walk?"

"If I have to."

"Sixty miles?" Sterling said in wonder. "And you can hardly get that thing across the room?"

Greystoke watched, very quiet.

Sterling moved toward her. "Let's talk it over," he said. "Let me try to explain everything."

"You can do that in your memoirs . . . I promise to buy a copy—paperback, of course."

"Is there any way I can make you change your mind?"

She paused by the door.

"Sure," she said. "Call your Pentagon and ask for reinforcements."

There were more than a dozen marines with artillery surrounding the cottage. Their commander stepped forward with a portable speaker. He barked into it, motioned the others, and six of them moved into the house pointing their rifles at Sterling and Melanie.

She closed her eyes in desperation. Two marines took Greystoke, who shrieked in protest. A corpsman with a medical insignia came up behind Greystoke, injected a tranquilizer, and the chimp strugged a few more seconds and collapsed on the floor. The marines lifted him and moved out quickly and efficiently.

"Are you Sterling Mann?" asked the commander.

Sterling nodded.

"Who is the girl?"

"The prisoner of Zenda," she said.

"All right, move," the commander ordered. "You are under arrest."

Sterling didn't move.

"Are we under military law?" he asked.

"Don't play smart ass, buddy," the officer said. "You broke into a security installation, kidnapped a cosmic classified experimental animal, and decoyed a few cars and personnel to their destruction."

"At least we know who we're dealing with here," Melanie said quaintly. "Nice, normal American soldiers!"

"I want to make a phone call," Sterling said.

"You want to call your lawyer?"

"No. Just the President of the United States."

CHAPTER TEN

Dr. Monroe was the first to greet Sterling as he landed in Washington.

"My boy," he began as they settled down after the initial greeting. It was a tone Sterling recognized, and he gave the doctor his full attention.

"Before you get into this . . . my boy, I have to tell you something very serious. I . . . I don't know quite how to begin . . ." His voice trailed off for a moment, then he said, "I feel you're coming to a very important point in your life. Something, I must confess, I had hoped would never happen. But it has all suddenly come into focus . . . curiously because of the murder of this young woman. It seems . . . very important now that you are about to talk to the . . . President. You should know everything. You should go fully equipped."

"Everything?" asked Sterling.

Dr. Monroe blew out a sigh and said nothing for a moment. He took a handkerchief from his breast pocket and mopped his brow and wiped his eyes. Then he launched into the Dease Lake experiment, sparing no details. Finally, when Dr. Monroe had finished, drained, Sterling sat very stiff, stunned. He had known there had been some kind of selective breeding involved in his conception but was not prepared for this.

At last Sterling said quietly, "So who . . . who were my parents?"

"Their names?"

"Their names."

"Sterling, I cannot . . . I should not . . . I will not tell you that. Anything else, but not that."

Dr. Monroe put his hand on Sterling's shoulder. "It is better this way, my boy. You should never know."

Sterling looked away toward the White House without really seeing it and slowly nodded. "You're right, I suppose. I should never know."

The very same day, as it happened, Sterling met one of his four fathers . . . and neither of them knew they were, in fact, father and son . . . and neither would ever know.

It happened in the Oval Office.

The President, young, arrogant, had flashed the famous smile and had turned on the spigot from which flowed the much vaunted Irish charm as the interview began. But Sterling was not buying it. Not only because Penelope's voice stress analyzer showed red for many of the President's statements, but because Sterling's own highly honed instincts told him that this man was, first and foremost, a politician.

And because the President was not stupid, he realized quickly that he was dealing with a superior intellect who wasn't to be patronized and he dropped the charm-boy act.

"Mr. Mann, I won't beat around the bush," he said in his Harvard accent, the cultivated public smile suddenly gone and his manner abruptly harsh. "FDR and the country did not spend all that money on you to produce a sort of playboy tycoon who takes things into his own hands, purely by whim it would appear."

Sterling flushed.

"Do you realize that due to you, Mr. Mann, and your misunderstanding of duty, a multimillion-dollar space laboratory, highly secretive and low profiled, was nearly blown?"

"It was a fluke, sir," said Sterling calmly. "A series of totally—"

"I will ask no questions about it!" said the President, bringing the flat of his hand down on the desk. "It is done, regrettably."

"If you have no questions for me," said Sterling. "I have some for you."

The command and force in Sterling's voice caused the President's eyes to widen.

"First, what was that gravity beam projector designed for? Second, why isn't the beam under the NASA banner and out in the open? Finally, was the death of Alexandra Robinson somehow tied in with that same project?"

The President leaned back in his chair, studying his poised and somewhat threatening visitor.

"Why should I tell you top-level secrets?" he asked laconically.

"Because I know something about them already," replied Sterling. "From the late Natasha Kern. And I'm sure you know who she was, Alexandra's friend."

The President shook his head. "We do not know that lady."

The regal use of "we" amused Sterling as he glanced down casually at Penelope and saw the red diodes appear. The President began to explain the bare bones of the project in his choppy, impatient sentences:

"Started with Carter and Brezhnev . . . when they met to discuss the SALT treaty . . . and, just incidentally, very much in private, the energy crisis. Result: nothing less than the first Russian-American joint scientific venture. Pretty good for a 'born again' moron, eh? Since then our scientists have been experimenting with atom and proton collisions, hoping, we've told the world, to discover the origins of matter, but in reality to discover an ultimate form of energy that would make gasoline immediately obsolete and eventually overwhelm the rag-heads."

"Rag-heads?" queried Sterling as naïvely as he could.

"The Arabs," said the President. "Wipe 'em out as a world power. We've kowtowed to them long enough. Anyway it was costly and slow and we weren't getting anywhere with the project until we got Alfreds to head it up. Heard of him? The wizard of science?"

"Stephen Balfour Alfreds," nodded Sterling. "Yale physics prof . . . one of the greatest. He's still alive?"

The President grinned as he pushed a buzzer, and Sterling realized for the first time how this man had always won such a great plurality at the polls.

"Send in Professor Alfreds, please," he said to apparently no one. Then to Sterling: "His ideas are too complicated for a physicistical dum-dum like me to explain, so I brought him here to do it for me."

Sterling only had time to speculate on what the *real* reason was that Alfreds had so conveniently been brought here, when a man appeared at the doorway to the big office. He was tall, and the first thing Sterling noticed was that he had a prominent hearing aid in both ears. Then he noticed the short gray beard, the erect carriage, and the sturdy stride for a man at least seventy. He was dressed in the shiny blue suit and bland red tie indifferently tied that is the uniform of the distinguished scientist everywhere.

"Professor Alfreds," said the President, "Sterling Mann."

As Sterling looked into the man's eyes, as black and darting and questing as a peregrine's, he felt some kind of emotion . . . he didn't know why or what, just his sixth sense trying to tell him something.

Obviously the older man felt something too, for he said, "Have we not met before?"

Sterling replied with great respect, "I would have remembered, sir. I know your work well, I have learned from you."

The scientist nodded; he was used to disciples acknowledging their debt to him. It meant little to him when they did. But if they were not to do it, it would mean a great deal to him.

The President clapped his hands together impatiently. "Alfreds, tell him about operation Nova as simply as possible."

"Well, to begin," said Alfreds, sinking into a leather chair, "and casting modesty to Aeolus, I believe my plan is the only solution to the world's problem. I have designed an accelerator of protons that doesn't limit itself to a couple miles of tunnels. To put it simple and in layman terms . . ."

"Don't feel you have to limit yourself in any way," said Sterling quietly, but Professor Alfreds seemed not to hear it. Sterling made a mental note to send him some information on the advances he had made with hearing systems—there was no need for him to be wearing those two old-fashioned devices.

"With laser beams . . . uh, ah, special methods I've devised," said Professor Alfreds. "With them I will shoot the protons up to a terminal in space, then send them speeding back to earth at four times the speed of light to a conventional tunnel where the magnets are maintained at freezing temperature and . . . are you understanding all this? I'm trying to keep it simple."

"I understand very well what you're talking about," said Sterling. "What happens after the collision is what interests me."

"The collision of the protons will be observed and studied by entirely new methods. The experiment will provide the earth and the free world with a solution"—the old man's eyes were bulging with the excitement of his project as though he were hyperthyroidal—"a triumphant solution to starvation and energy! Imagine . . . free energy for everyone emanating from matter itself!"

Alfreds looked at Sterling expectantly, awaiting his reply. The President was also studying Sterling.

"Well, what do you think, Mann?"

Sterling stood up and walked a few steps across the heavy carpet, shaking his head. Then he turned.

"With all due respect, sir," he said. "Couldn't this experiment backfire?"

"Backfire?" asked Alfreds incredulously. He was not used to his ideas being questioned.

"Such acceleration of protons . . . well, it's frightening. What if they get out of control?"

"Young man," said the professor coldly, "you think I don't know what I'm doing, that I haven't thought of control?"

"Well, of course," said Sterling respectfully, "It's just . . . how can one control such an experiment? What if the collision results in a matter-antimatter explosion that would wipe out the entire laboratory, maybe even the entire area, and then ultimately destroy all the surrounding space?"

Alfreds stood up stiffly. "I do not suffer fools gladly! I would not tolerate such impertinence from even my own son! I would not have come here today had not the President of the United States requested me to. I think I have complied, and I shall now depart and return to the world of qualified scientists. Good day to you. Good day, Mr. President!"

After he had gone Sterling felt a pang as he watched the man walk to the door. He had not meant to alienate this brilliant man who probably had only the highest motives and goals. But, damnit, he, too, knew something about the subject, and he could not sit silent when something so lethal and important could become a reality. The

President swiveled himself around so that his back was to Sterling.

"Mr. President," Sterling began, "I did not intend any slight on Professor Alfreds's experiment. It's just that it seems to me to be very arrogant and risky—"

The President swung around in his chair and his Irish eyes were blazing. He had a yellow pencil in his hand, and he kept tapping his lips with it angrily as he spoke.

"It is you, Mr. Mann, who are both arrogant and a risk. And, I might add, a bit of an embarrassment and anachronistic. You might have been necessary when FDR dreamed you up so long ago, but I am not so sure you are needed in the scheme of things today."

Sterling ignored this and said quietly, "What, Mr. President, may I ask, is the reason you are backing this dangerous project, this Nova experiment, so wholeheartedly and so blindly? Is your target a genuine one? To save the world from its energy crisis? Or is it possibly politically motivated so that you may remain securely in this pleasant oval-shaped office?"

The President bit into the middle of the pencil.

"Mr. Mann, you haven't responded to my previous statement—that you are obsolescent and perhaps expendable."

"Am I to understand that I am, as of now, in effect, fired?" Sterling said with a smile.

"If I could," said the President. "I would do it

with pleasure. But alas, it was set up in such a way that neither I nor any subsequent President can do that."

Sterling got up from his chair.

"I must catch a plane. Good-bye, sir. It was edifying, if unsettling."

"It was that," said the President, brusquely, not rising and not raising his head from the letters on his desk that he had begun to sign.

CHAPTER ELEVEN

Melanie awakened and looked around. For a moment everything seemed strange to her and then she remembered. She was in her sister's apartment. The hectic events of the ordeal in Connecticut, the wild chase with poor Greystoke finally being overpowered by soldiers, her bitter words to Sterling, and her profound relief when she was at last returned to Alexandra's apartment all washed over her in instant replay, as she lay there waiting to get the energy to arise.

She had a busy day ahead, perhaps her last in New York. The attorneys had arranged for her to meet the bankers, and there were other details to be attended to. She always had thought that death was only a sad affair, now she was discovering that death, for relatives of people with money, was also a very complicated affair, too.

She'd go back to her students, and never, never think of New York again. Never think of Sterling again. It wasn't easy, but she would at least try. She felt like a fool, the way she had behaved to Sterling. She and her wrong timing.

A bell sounded. Was it the telephone? No, the doorbell. She jumped up, put on her robe, and went to the door.

"Who is it?"

"Jess . . . doorman here. Brought Miss Alexandra's mail, miss." Melanie opened the door and took the sheaf of letters from him. "Thank you," she said.

She looked through the letters quickly. Somehow she had the feeling that she might find something connected to Alexandra's death.

Ten minutes later she had given up. Nothing but credit-card bills, two letters from Alexandra's publishers, checks for residuals, and a telephone bill.

She looked at the telephone bill once more and this time she noticed an entry for $58.80 for one call. She had called Gilgit? Where the hell was Gilgit? Sterling would have to come up with an answer immediately. No, she thought, no more calls to Sterling. But then, who else? Who else was really interested? She realized how very alone she was now. And how vulnerable.

She telephoned Sterling's apartment to apologize.

Nicholas told her, "Mr.-Sterling's-at-the-stock-exchange-miss," in his electronic voice.

Stock exchange! She gave a little laugh. It seemed so incongruous with Sterling's flamboyant life-style of the last few days. But of course he was an inventor and a car manufacturer, hence a businessman, so he'd have to know about and deal with the stock exchange.

She dressed quickly.

An hour later Sterling, down on the floor of the Exchange surrounded by the havoc of agents buying and selling, looked up to see, across the crowd, someone waving papers agitatedly over her head. It was Melanie! He had thought he'd never see her again. Now she was signing to him that she was sorry. Then, "Must talk to you right now," she signed as the people around her watched curiously.

Sterling quickly concluded his business with his broker and made his way to Melanie. She showed him the phone bill.

Sterling checked with Penelope. "Gilgit, small town in Himalayas, latitude three hundred and sixty degrees, longitude seventy-three degrees, northwest Kashmir," came the sparse information from the computer. "Population is Muslim, mainly of the Shia sect and—"

"That's enough, thank you, dear." He gestured to an empty office cubicle nearby. "My broker's," he said, following Melanie in. Sterling placed a call to the Gilgit number.

While they sat and waited for the call, Melanie asked, "Why that strange place? Who would she know way out in the middle of nowhere?"

Sterling shrugged casually, but inwardly he felt an excitement, sensing that he was closer to the solution of the mystery than he had ever been.

The call came in half an hour. Sterling heard a voice that was surprisingly clear, as though from New Jersey rather than the Himalayas, uttering a stream of words in the singsong Shia language. This was one language that Sterling had not learned.

"Do you speak English?" he asked. "Chinese, Arabic, Sanskrit?"

There was a pause. Then a cautious, "Yes, En-grish."

"Who are you?"

"Clerk in Hotel Karakoram Hotel."

"Ah, good," said Sterling. "I got your right number. May I . . . may I speak with Alexandra Robinson, please."

"Miss Robinson not here . . . not arrive until fourth."

"But she has a reservation?"

"Oh, most surely."

"Thank you very much," said Sterling. "I will call back then, in two days." He hung up.

"So we are going to the Himalayas," said Melanie.

"*I* am going to the Himalayas," he replied.

"Not this time," she said. "It is *my* information, after all."

"I'll travel faster alone," he said. "And it might be rough out there."

"And what would you call the last few days?" Then she said, "Look, at the hotel they obviously don't know that Alexandra is dead."

"Obviously."

"And equally obviously Alexandra was going halfway around the world to meet someone very important. That someone also probably doesn't know that Alexandra is dead yet."

"So if you posed as Alexandra . . ." Sterling mused, "and showed up there day after tomorrow, they might . . ."

"Right!" she said. "And for a genius, you think pretty slow. They, whoever they are, would get in touch with me."

Sterling contacted Penelope. "Connecting flights to Gilgit . . . soonest departure. For two."

"Yes, sir," said Penelope.

"And, Penelope," Sterling added, not really expecting any information, "in your data on Gilgit is there any possible reason that could cause Alexandra Robinson to go there?"

"WTK, sorry," Penelope flashed back.

Almost as soon as the Air India 747 took off, Melanie, tired by the frantic packing and rush for the airport, fell asleep in her seat. Sterling put her head gently on a pillow, covered her with a blan-

ket, then took his book, *The Mysterious Himalayas*, and went from the first-class section up the
spiral stairs to the lounge.

He was the only person in the comfortable, den-
like compartment, and he relaxed on one of the
sofas. He looked out the window . . . it was already dark. He put a pillow behind his head. It
would be a long, long flight with several plane
changes. He started to read his book but he felt
himself dozing.

"Mind if I join you up here, sir?" said an English
accent.

Sterling opened his eyes to see an elegantly
dressed, rotund gentleman in front of him. The fat
red cheeks looked almost rouged, and the open
smile and ingenuous blue eyes were those of a
child trying to ingratiate himself into a world of
grown-ups.

Sterling nodded and the Englishman, wheezing
slightly, lowered his bulk down into the over-
stuffed chair next to the sofa. He took out the
gold watch whose chain was strung across his protruding tweed vest and clucked.

"Oh, dearie me, what a long ways we have to
go, eh? What time, sir, would you guess it was in
Kashmir?"

"Ah, you're off to Kashmir," said Sterling,
glancing at his watch, and Penelope digitally
showed him what time it was in Gilgit.

"I'd guess around nine forty-five A.M.," said
Sterling.

"Good of you," said the man, looking a little surprised that Sterling would have that information so quickly as he changed his watch. "Like to get on m' destination's local time soon as possible. By the by," he said extending his hand, "m' name's A. Morley Houseman, at your service, as m' dad used to say."

Sterling felt like replying, "And for short should I call you A?" but he took the man's pudgy hand with fingers like five white sausages and said, "Sterling Mann. And what, may I ask, *is* your destination?"

"Like you, first Katmandu. Remember dear Rudyard's line"—he waved his fat hand airily in what was meant to be a poetic gesture—" 'And the wildest dreams of Kew are the facts of Katmandu.' "

"And then?"

The man gave a great sigh of weariness. "Oh my, so many places, dreary places . . . Delhi, Lahore, Jodhpur, Jaipur, and even, God help me, even Rawalpindi."

"And Gilgit?"

"And even little Gilgit, but mercifully briefly, in that carbuncle on the anus of creation. Been there?"

"No," replied Sterling, wanting to get back to his book. "And what takes you to those out of the way spots?"

"The CAUC. I work for the CAUC. Of course, you've heard of the CAUC?"

Sterling looked blank.

"Don't blame you . . . Cultural Advancement for Undeveloped Countries." He gave a chuckle that was more of a giggle. "England's last desperate attempt to pass on all our fatuous Victorian notions to the wogs. Stripped of our colonies, we must go bare-assed into the fields of the Lord."

Pushing back his lapel, from the array of pens in his vest pocket he pulled out one. "My calling card, a present from the England of the past to a citizen of one of her former colonies."

Sterling looked at the black pen a moment. In gold on the side was written: "Courtesy of CAUC."

"Not a bad pen at all," said the Englishman, "considering"—he held his right hand to the side of his face in a conspiratorial manner— "considering how cheaply we get them made for us in Japan! The natives everywhere go mad for them. Much better, more effective than the glass beads and nails old Captain Cook used to use!"

"Thanks," said Sterling. He put the pen in his breast pocket and stood up. "If you'll excuse me, I'll go see how my traveling companion is."

The Englishman looked up, smiled his beatific choirboy smile, and almost whispered, "As we say in the Himalayas . . . *à bientôt, monsieur.*"

"Gilgit," said Melanie as they walked through the dirty, crowded marketplace. The twilight air was filled with the pungent smells of the foods and wet wool and strange music. "So this is gorgeous downtown Gilgit! If you could but know the times I've yearned to get away from my job and come to lovely . . ."

"Look over there," said Sterling quietly, touching her arm.

Through the stalls of fruit and meat, woolen goods, and brass artifacts he had caught a glimpse of the fat Englishman's tweed hat.

"What?" asked Melanie.

"The man who was on the same plane as ours from New York," said Sterling.

Sterling casually guided Melanie around the corner of a little restaurant, then stopped and waited. In a few moments the Englishman came around the corner fast, surprisingly for such a corpulent man. He looked a little startled, then said, "Oh, hullo!" Cheerily, very cheerily, *"Thought* I saw you. How d'ye do, ma'am? how's Gilgit striking you?"

"Fine," said Sterling, pleasantly. "Pleasant meeting you here. I thought you said you had to go to all those other cities first? Or did I misunderstand?"

"Decided I'd get Gilgit out of the way soon as possible . . . can't stand the bloody place . . ." He gestured exasperatedly at the great mountains around the town, now bathed in a roseate glow that made them look as though they were made from raspberry sherbet. "Hate the bloody hills, remind me of . . . Switzerland. Staying at the Hotel Gilgit, are you?"

"There's another?"

"Right you are, limited choice, eh what?" He took out a card which read "A. Morley House-man" and underneath, "CAUC."

"Maybe we might have a drink . . . in the bar? Hotel . . . later . . . eh?" He tipped his hat and waddled off.

"Hmmm," mused Melanie as she watched him go.

"What does that enigmatic sound mean?"

"Well, he was clearly following us, wasn't he? Wonder what Fatty is up to."

"I would imagine," said Sterling solemnly, "that he's up to about two hundred fifty pounds."

"Damn you, Sterling. I can never tell what you are really thinking! Why is that man following us? Sure, we made it abundantly clear around the hotel's bar and restaurant that I was Alexandra Robinson, but you tell me he was on the plane. Why would he follow us all the way from New York?"

"Who's to know?" said Sterling. "Let's go back to the hotel and see if anyone's risen to the bait."

Sterling was awakened in the middle of that night unpleasantly; he had the distinct impression that the cold object being pressed against his neck was a sharp blade. The bedside lamp was snapped on and Sterling saw that it was indeed the blade of a *gorkha* hatchet-knife called a *rukri,* and the wielder had a knee on either side of Sterling's body. He was an awesome sight. A giant of a man with a full brown beard, thick brows pasted over two huge eyes as black as charcoal briquets, dressed like a mountain climber. His mouth was moving but Sterling, having removed Penelope when he went to bed, couldn't understand what he was saying. He could get some of the words by lip reading, but it was difficult as the man obviously had an accent.

"Who this girl?" Sterling made out as the man jerked his hand toward Melanie, who had been sleeping on her stomach and was just beginning to stir.

"Alexandra Robinson," Sterling answered, "and I am—"

"Lie!" the man's lips said. "Alexandra dead! You, too, if you lie again!"

At this moment Melanie lifted her head and saw the apparition crouched over Sterling. She screamed and the giant glanced over at her, growling, "You no make noise, woman!"

In the split second that the man took his eyes off him, Sterling jerked his head to the left, away from the blade, and at the same time delivered a smashing blow with the side of his hand to the giant's huge right forearm. The hatchet flew from his grasp and clattered on the floor as Sterling flipped off the bed and onto his feet.

With a great bellow the big man clambered off the bed and charged at Sterling. Since the man was coming at him headfirst and in a crouch with his arms lowered in a grappling position, Sterling hit him with a conventional boxing combination—two fast left jabs and a tremendous right to the face. The man was slammed back to the floor, a surprised expression on his face and a trickle of blood at the corner of his mouth. But he got up and charged; and this time he came so fast and hard that Sterling barely had time to get off 'one punch before being smashed back up against the wall. The giant's fists were pounding his ribs like pneumatic hammers. Sterling brought his knee up hard into the other's groin, and when the man threw back his head in pain, Sterling slashed his right hand into the exposed adam's apple. Two more devastating blows, one to the temple and the other to the point of the huge man's chin, and it was all over. The Himalayan Paul Bunyan crumpled, sagged to his knees, and fell over to one side.

"Well," panted Sterling, "I've fought better boxers, but never bigger ones."

He walked over to the night table and strapped on Penelope. Melanie kneed herself across the bed and curled her arms around Sterling's waist, her head against his bare chest.

"David," she whispered. "My own private David."

Sterling put on his bathrobe, got a glass of water from the bathroom, and sloshed it on the face of the supine Goliath. He shook his head, groaned, and opened his eyes.

"You good fighter, Mr. Mann," he said with no

animosity. "Nobody ever beat Arkassi before." He sprang up and bent his great hulk in a ludicrous jerky bow.

"*Namas-te,*" he said in Sanskrit. "I salute you."

"You know my name."

"I know you name, sah," Then he pointed to Melanie. "I no know her name. No Alexandra. Alexandra dead."

"I'm her sister," said Melanie.

"Sister," said Arkassi appraising her. "You good-looking sister. I not know Alexandra, but you good-lookin'!"

"Thank you," said Melanie.

"Alexandra, she hire me . . . best tam guide in Kashmir . . . I s'pose take her Gorak Shep."

"And where is that?" asked Sterling.

Arkassi rolled his eyes heavenward enigmatically and pointed up. "High!"

"Why did she want to go to Gorak . . ." Melanie hesitated. "Is it Shep? Why there?"

"I no know . . . all I know, she send money, I get expedition ready to go Gorak Shep—Sherpas, everything. Now no boss man, sahib, how you say . . . client."

"We'll go," said Melanie.

"Better you no go," Arkassi said. "Sahib go. You stay. Danger."

"But you were going to take my sister!" protested Melanie.

Arkassi shook his shaggy head. "Rain, avalanche

come since. Trails no good. Ver' much danger. Arkassi got family look out for you, protect you. Sahib back soon."

"I come all this way just to sit in Gilgit!" fumed Melanie. "Damn, damn, damn! And 'sahib' yet! Just like all those old movies! What you need is a memsahib . . . I can drive a Jeep!"

Arkassi laughed. "Memsahib, only wheel between here and Gorak Shep—*prayer* wheel!"

It was a closed issue with Arkassi. He took Sterling's hand in both of his massive ones and shook it vigorously, "Sah, I get all men ready . . . we leave six in morning."

"Tell me, Arkassi," said Sterling. "What is in Gorak Shep that would lure Alexandra Robinson there?"

The big man looked uncomfortable. "Nothing in Gorak Shep."

"Nothing?"

The man remained silent, then blurted out, "Only the Healer!" before turning and lurching out of the room.

The Healer . . . it meant nothing to Sterling, but he felt an instinctive trust in Arkassi and that he would lead them to the core of the mystery.

His confidence was not shared by Melanie, whose awareness that she was to be left alone in an outpost of the Himalayas drove all possibility of sleep from her mind. She looked at his fine profile, his pleasantly rugged face, which was close to being too handsome when he smiled but now, in sleep, was almost boyish and innocent. She realized how much she depended upon him, trusted him, and needed him. Disturbing thoughts for one so accustomed to being independent . . . to being needed by others. Finally the soft regularity of his breathing soothed her fears, and she snuggled against his chest and fell asleep.

A vulturous brown griffon swung lazily in arcs above them, an enormous bowl of snow stretched out below them, and towering above was the great mountain of Sortaspur with its Shandur Pass, the gateway to Gorak Shep.

Arkassi stood defiantly surveying the panorama. Then he gestured at the mountain and bellowed, "Sah, now you see great mounting . . . great dwelling of snow. 'Him' mean snow, 'alaya' mean dwelling. We, how you say, we win him . . ." He shook his fist at the mountain. "We . . ."

"We'll conquer him," said Sterling.

"You tam right, sah!" agreed Arkassi.

A dark red and black fox ran across the path in front of him and disappeared into the rocks and snow with a flash of its white-tipped tail.

"Hey, you see 'im? 'Im good luck. We get Gorak Shep, no trouble!"

Despite his great size, Arkassi proved to be as sure-footed as the blue-silver-gray goats, the rare bharal, by the side of the trail as he led the expedition up the mountain. Behind him on the two-foot-wide trail came Sterling with a rucksack, and

following came four Sherpas, their foreheads bent
forward against the straps attached to their loads,
which at any moment threatened to bump against
the wall of the mountain and nudge them over the
precipice to crash on the rocks of the Ghizar River
so many hundreds of feet below them.

At one point on that first day the trail was so
narrow and the wind so strong that they had to
get down on their hands and knees for a mile. Another time Arkassi did not see a protruding shelf
of ice at his head level and received a glancing
but sharp blow as he walked into it. Although it
didn't cut him, he was stunned and he swayed
precariously for a moment until Sterling leaped
forward and pinned the big body to the mountain
side of the trail. He came to his senses almost immediately and hugged Sterling, like a little boy, in
gratitude.

A later incident happened at five thousand feet
when Sterling was about to cross a snow bridge
arching over a crevice and Arkassi grabbed him
before the first step. With his staff Arkassi prodded the snow and the bridge collapsed. It was
Sterling's turn to thank Arkassi.

Later, over their dinner that night at dusk, their
breath showing like steam in the firelight, they
had a good talk. Sterling told Arkassi about the
western world. Arkassi told Sterling about the Himalayas. Sterling asked if Arkassi would like to see
other parts of the world, and Arkassi looked long
into the fire, then said, "How can a tree travel?"

He took several bites of *dhal* and a sip of *so-cha*, his buttered tea, and continued, "I have roots like a tree. When the winds blow me, I can lean to the east or to the west, but I cannot leave the soil my roots grow in. I pull up my roots, I die. This"—he gestured around at the mountains—"this my country, my roots here."

Sterling nodded, reflecting upon his own origins, and said quietly, "I guess it is a good feeling to have roots."

Together they silently finished their *chapati* bread and yak cheese. Then Arkassi produced a bottle from his rucksack and two cups.

"*Raki!*" he proclaimed with a provocative leer and an exaggerated moistening of his thick lips. "You hear of our 'Promise of Heaven,' eh?" He guffawed. "Made from innocent rice."

Sterling hadn't, but one brief sip told him that it did indeed promise heaven, but perhaps also oblivion on the way and purgatory after. He put the cup down.

After three *rakis*, Arkassi was in an expansive mood, and he talked about his great love for the mountains.

Sterling listened as Arkassi talked. It was dark now, very dark, and Sterling didn't know that stars had ever been so numerous and large and sharp-edged . . . they seemed to be pasted on an ultramarine blue sky that was almost black in this dustless, smogless atmosphere.

Arkassi told how his father, "the greates' mountain man of all," had wandered to Gilgit from a Russian border town, met a Sherpa girl and married her, and became a famous guide until a fatal avalanche.

"Now," said Arkassi with no boastfulness, "I am greates' guide. But you save Arkassi's life today." He gave a stentorian laugh. "So now maybe you greates', sah!"

"Speaking of greatest," said Sterling. "Who is this great Healer that you mentioned? Do you think he's the one Alexandra wanted to see?"

Arkassi scowled and shook his head. "I never speak to this Alexandra Robinson."

"How did she contact you?"

"Hotel say when she call she want guide. Hotel always call me. Like I tell you, Arkassi greates' guide!"

Arkassi had been as good as his word when he said that he would have someone in his family look after Melanie.

Shortly after Sterling had left with Arkassi and the Sherpas, Melanie was called by the room clerk to let her know that Arkassi's sister had arrived.

"Send her up, please," said Melaine.

At the knock she opened the door to see the enormous bosom of a giantess. Kaala was almost as tall as Arkassi and much wider. Melanie looked up into a round, open face with a grin much like Arkassi's. The woman strode into the room laughing and nodding, and Melanie gestured to a chair.

She immediately liked this Asian Amazon and found herself laughing and nodding in return.

Melanie made motions of eating to indicate that she would like to have breakfast. Kaala gave a good-natured chuckle and nodded. She stood up and beckoned to Melanie to follow her. With her great bosom proudly extended in front of her, the broad shoulders well back, she regally made her way out the room and down to the street. Melanie felt sure that this woman would know good food and where to get it.

Together they walked through the streets of Gilgit, past the stalls of the bazaar. Melanie pointed to a lovely jade bracelet and smiled at Kaala. The big woman laughed and nodded as Melanie bought it and put it on.

Suddenly a stout figure came toward them. He was not dressed like most of the mountain people in the thick felt coats, the pajama trousers, felt hat rolled up at the edges, cloth puttees, and boots; he was clothed more as though from a monastery, in a loose garment with a cowl that almost hid his face. He was carrying a small black box.

"Missy," said a heavily accented voice, "you buy bad jewelry, no real jade! You get real jade, real stones here, this place." He produced a printed card with exotic writing on it that Melanie could not read, but under which was written in ink, "Palace of Jade, Hindu Kush St. Center of Gilgit."

Kaala looked on in disapproval, the smile gone

from her face, but she did not understand the pidgin English. She had never seen this man before, and she could not determine whether or not he was part of Melanie's group of "foreigners."

Melanie said, "I'm really not interested in expensive—"

"Look!" he interrupted. "Look how much pretty than you bracelet is this jade ring. You take . . . how you call . . . sample. Tomorrow you come my place, see real jewelry." He shoved the card and the ring into her hand, then turned and scuttled away.

Melanie showed the ring to Kaala. Kaala looked at it admiringly, no longer worried. Obviously the man who gave it to Melanie was a friend of hers.

They were soon at the café where Kaala and Melanie were to have breakfast. As Kaala was ordering the food, a man dressed as a Sherpa reeled drunkenly against Melanie, bumped her hard, mumbled something in apology, and staggered off. Kaala turned and saw him as he stumbled away and started to give chase, but Melanie caught her arm and shook her head. Kaala sat down and was soon her happy, laughing self as she and Melanie began to eat the melon that was brought to them. Then Kaala pointed to Melanie's finger. The ring was no longer there. Melanie realized then that the drunken man had skillfully removed it in her confusion. Kaala was again ready to give chase, but it was too late. The man had had too much time and was well away. Gradually

Melanie calmed the outraged Kaala and they finished their breakfast.

The fat Englishman watched them from the shadows of a side street. When they settled down and seemed absorbed in their food, he pushed back the cowl of his monastic disguise, opened the black box, and withdrew a bat. In a trice he had removed its hood and launched it into the air. But to his amazement it flew not toward the table where Melanie and Kaala sat but banked sharply to the left and disappeared down an alley. Just then Melanie looked his way, and although she did not see him, he knew he had better get away, and slipped back into the shadow of the buildings, still trying to catch sight of his wayward bat.

The man who had bumped into Melanie, walking now without a stagger and perfectly sober, was just about to enter a doorway and greet his "fence" when the bat caught up with him.

When he opened the door and lurched into the office of Gilgit's leading expert in the disposal of stolen goods, the man indeed appeared to be drunk.

"Why you come here like this?" asked the fence angrily.

The thief had barely the strength to hold out the ring and gasp, "How much you . . ." before falling to the floor.

The next day, once through the pass, the trail leveled off and the going was easier, although one

Sherpa fell six feet through an ice bridge and would have plunged to his death if Arkassi had not luckily been close enough to grab his pack and haul the babbling man back up. They were delayed more than half a day and Arkassi promised to make it up, but Sterling was not worried, for there was no indication that they were being followed.

In the afternoon they came to open snow-covered meadows set down in the hollow at the base of the enormous mountains. It was a good place to camp and they pitched the tents in the fading light.

"Someone else think it ver' nice place," said Arkassi. He was scanning the terrain with Sterling's miniature binoculars; the big man was fascinated with the extraordinarily powerful no-hips roof-prism glasses that Mann Industries had recently begun to market.

Sterling made out a group of tiny dark figures against the snow, far behind them. They were setting up tents on a level part of the meadow. He took the glasses and adjusted them so that he could see the Sherpas' faces below their woolen hats. And then he saw an incongruously fat, pink face such as no Sherpa had ever possessed on a rotund body dressed in the usual Himalayan climbing clothes.

He handed the glasses back to Arkassi. "You keep them. They're yours."

Arkassi looked at him incredulously. "You give these Arkassi? No need?"

"I've seen what I wanted to see," said Sterling.

Arkassi hugged the glasses to his heart like a little boy with a new toy.

After dinner Arkassi drank his usual amount of *raki* and soon was snoring by the fire. Sterling made sure the pen was in his parka, then he removed an object wrapped in brown wax paper from his rucksack, and as silent as a cobra on the snow, he set off down the meadow. In the moonlight, which glazed everything blue-silver, he could see the other camp and the largest tent. The lamps had been blown out, and only the coals of the fire showed that people were there.

He came up to the tent warily and pulled back the flap. The moonlight revealed the fat torso of the Englishman protruding from his down sleeping bag. Sterling entered the tent and crouched over the snoring man's form for a moment.

As Sterling stood up, the Englishman rolled over, gave several snorts, and suddenly sat up, flipping on a powerful lantern by his sleeping bag as he did.

"Hold everything right there, Mr. Mann," said the cultivated tones, and Sterling could see that he was clutching a snub-nosed pistol that was pointed at Sterling's chest. He raised his hands.

"What an honor," the man went on, "to entertain the redoubtable Mr. Mann, even under such primitive conditions as these. And even so briefly as this interview. And I assure you that it will be brief, Mr. Mann, regrettably brief. Mercifully brief, if you will."

"Before we, ah terminate our little visit, Mister . . . Mister . . . ?"

"Mr. Ellenshaw. Yes, I rather like that one. F. Winston Ellenshaw . . . never used that one before, like it a lot."

"May one ask, before one is shot or whatever you intend to do to me, who you are, Mr. Ellenshaw? Who do you work for? Why did you kill Alexandra? And why did you follow me for ten thousand miles to keep me from getting to Gorak Shep?"

"Ah, the sweet mysteries of life, eh, Mr. Mann? Suffice it to say that I am for hire, and just who hired me in this case will concern you not at all five minutes from now. Nothing, you see, will concern you a whit in five minutes."

He got out of the sleeping bag, never taking his eyes off Sterling for an instant, never lowering the gun barrel from the level of his opponent's chest. He padded over to the corner of the tent where there was a large box with holes in it.

"But you should know that there is nothing for you to be ashamed of . . . you have fallen to an expert. Trained originally by the British Secret Service y'know, I have become unique, an artist in my field. One of a kind . . . I deal with crime, with contracts, as carefully and conscientiously as a diamond cutter approaching a rough cut on a priceless stone. My trade, and there are precious few of us left, has been severely maligned and lessened by all these terrorists, the CIA, the KGB . . . supermarkets of death I call them. I, my dear Mr. Mann, have style and class. You may say that I am running my own 'Boutique of Crime'—catchy title, wot, for m' memoirs. Family operation, y'see . . . my wife, my son, myself. No violence, no unnecessary explosions to pollute the air, no noise." His eyes glittered expectantly as his fingers wandered to the door of the box. "Handmade weapons, y'might say, like these . . . my little colleagues . . . trained to follow subsonic signals, conditioned little by little to be immune to curare. Look at them."

He put down the pistol as he opened the door, and seven vampire bats flew out and silently and wildly zigzagged around the tent, the light from the lantern casting their huge surrealistic shadows onto the canvas as the fat man chortled delightedly.

"Good-bye, Mr. Mann," he said with a smile as the bats prepared to attack.

"Good-bye to you, Mr. Ellenshaw," said Sterling with an equally pleased smile. "And thanks for the pen. It didn't write very well so I returned it to you."

The smile on the Englishman's face faded, his hand went up to his pocket, and his fingers just had time to touch the pen that shone there and his expression went into a horror mask as the bats dropped down from the top of the tent like dive-bombers, biting him on the face and neck and skull.

At the same time Sterling unwrapped the object in his hand. It looked like a cordless hair dryer, but when he pressed a button, a tongue of flame licked out from it with a roar. A few short bursts charcoaled the bats, and Sterling backed out as the flames jumped to the walls of the tent.

As he made his way quickly across the snow back to his encampment, he could hear the excited yells of the Sherpas as they fought the fire.

And then what had been bothering him for some time suddenly hit him with full force: How had the Englishman, and God knows how many other people, known his every movement? How had the Englishman known he was going to Marrakesh, where he was staying, and so forth? How had he known about Gilgit and Gorak Shep? Only Nicholas and Dr. Monroe knew his movements. Nicholas . . . a fink? Impossible, he had been with him forever and was entirely trustworthy. Dr. Monroe? Unthinkable.

There was no one else . . . except Melanie. Could she have deceived him from the beginning? After all he didn't know much about her. She just "happened" to be hitchhiking on the highway. Who else knew he was heading for Gorak Shep . . . and what awaited him there?

"Gottam!" exclaimed Arkassi, pointing. "You got Koka!"

He reached for one of the three cans of Coco-Cola on the top of Sterling's other supplies. Sterling grabbed the man by his thick wrist in a powerful grip before the fingers could touch the metal can.

"Hey!" said Arkassi angrily. "What's matter? I not good enough for you Koka?"

Still holding the man's wrist away from the red cans, Sterling said quietly, "Arkassi, it is not that." He smiled then and said, "Koka is not good enough for *you*, Arkassi. Tea is much better for both of us."

Sterling released the man's wrist and, puzzled, Arkassi accepted the substitute drink.

Suddenly a shadow fell across the table. Sterling looked up and saw a tall, buxom girl-woman looking down at him. She could have been any age between sixteen and twenty. Unlike the other chignoned women in the village, her hair was loose and swirled around her face. Her wild black eyes were Asian, but the other features were not, and her skin was the color of Sterling's. She was a striking contrast to the other women he had seen in this land, what with her height, beauty, and the bulging red blouse under the chamois jacket above the black trousers. She had a large silver knife sheath on her belt.

She spoke rapidly in a tongue Sterling could not understand.

"She say her name Lafia. She welcome us to village," Arkassi said, translating. "She say her father head man of village . . . he very sick . . . you come quick, she say."

Could the old man Arkassi spoke of possibly have a daughter this young?

Sterling said, "Who is your father?" and Arkassi translated.

"They call him the Healer. Now it is he who must be healed. Come, please come."

"I am not a doctor."

"But you are more of a doctor than anyone in this town!"

Sterling shook his head. "I studied only a little premed."

"He is dying!" Then, seeing that Sterling still showed some reluctance, she said under her breath, "My father . . . has a story to tell you . . . a very important story."

Sterling got up from the table quickly and Arkassi followed. Lafia went down the main street at a fast walk, almost a trot. The girl was not quite six feet tall, yet she looked like a giantess compared to the small, flat-chested women of the village. At the end of the street she turned to the right onto a rocky path with melting snow like patches of wet cotton. The path led steeply up the hill to two small stone cottages.

Lafia pulled the latch thong of the largest cottage and the thick wooden door creaked open. She stepped inside and the two men followed. It was dark inside the room, especially after the bright afternoon sun, but Sterling's superior vision quickly made out the crude table, a yak skin on the floor, a pair of chamois horns on one wall, and the rest all clean and neat and bare except for another wall that was floor to ceiling stacked with books—huge old books that looked like medical and scientific tomes. In and around the books were empty bottles.

For a moment Sterling didn't see the pallet in the corner with a form on it under the fur coverlet. Then Lafia lit a lamp and beckoned to him. Sterling walked over and looked down at the sick man.

The bald head sticking out under the blanket looked like that of a Galapagos turtle protruding from its shell. His eyes were partially open but not seeing, his mouth a gelid rictus, his breathing shallow and barely making the coverlet rise and fall. His face was lined, the cheek bones sharp, the eyes sunken. But this was clearly not the hundred-year-old man Arkassi had mentioned. He appeared to be about sixty-five at the most.

His daughter knelt down by him, moistened his lips with a damp cloth in a bowl by his head, and looked up beseechingly at Sterling for help. Sterling dropped to one knee, took off Penelope, and passed it over the head of the supine man while asking her silently, "How old is this person?"

After an almost instantaneous analysis of the bone structure, the dental and skin tissues, the readout on the watch came back: "Between one hundred and two and one hundred and four."

Amazed, Sterling reacted with: "Are you sure?"

"I do not make snap judgments," the readout said.

"And with such a young daughter?"

"Love recognizes no age barriers."

"That is good to know," Sterling replied, but before he could ask her about the old man's specific ailments, Arkassi touched his arm and said, "I think his sickness is there." He pointed to the empty bottles by the books. "He got *raki* sickness. Him bottom of flask."

Sterling looked at him questioningly.

"In Himalayas," Arkassi said, "man is born with full flask . . . flask of life, we say. Slower he drink, more he last." He pointed at himself and gave his gravelly laugh. "Me . . . I got half flask left. Him . . . he drink his life to bottom. No one can save him. He now got to drop empty flask and go to fountain of eternal life."

"Curious, you in your country say 'drop the flask' and we say 'kick the bucket.'"

"Kick the bucket!" repeated Arkassi, delighted with the new phrase. "Well, this one . . . he going to kick the bucket."

Sterling said to Penelope, "Specific bodily irregularities, please," and he slowly began moving the watch, scanning the entire figure. In a few moments Penelope reported: "Can find few imperfections. Only major ailment cirrhotic due to chronic ingestion of pure ethanol."

Sterling turned to Arkassi. "You were right . . . liver trouble, too much flask." Then to Penelope: "What do you recommend?"

"Right now, considering situation, conditions, geographical location, very little."

"That's a big help. There must be something I can try."

"Acupuncture."

"But I have no needles," said Sterling. "How is acupuncture possible with no needles?"

The readout was slow in coming back, but soon it said, "What about LHLP?"

Sterling felt inside his jacket and made sure the low-helium laser pen he always carried was there.

"Good girl!"

"Thank you."

When Lafia saw Sterling take out the pen and move toward her father, she instinctively drew the dagger from the sheath at her belt. Sterling saw its glint in the dim light and tried to smile reassuringly at her.

"Tell her," he said to Arkassi, "tell her I'm only trying to help him."

"So he don't kick bucket," Arkassi added and translated for the girl. She nodded but her beautiful eyes remained hard and watchful and the dagger was not returned to its sheath.

Sterling pressed the button on the head of the

pen and the tiny, dazzling needle of light stabbed out of the pointed end. He turned the ring that circled the barrel of the pen and adjusted the wavelength. Soon he had an instrument that functioned similarly to an acupuncture needle. Then he turned it off and pulled back the fur coverlet. He had expected a living skeleton and was surprised to see that the old man, while thin, had a muscular, sturdy torso. Only the slightest bulge under the rib cage on the right side revealed the liver damage.

He soon found the first place on the forearm, turned on the light, and inserted "the needle." He held it there for a long moment, turning the pen. The beam penetrated the tissue better than any needle, with no bleeding. Then he withdrew the beam and moved it to another neural center in the trapezius muscle behind the neck.

Five more anatomical locations were probed as Arkassi watched in wonderment and Lafia with skepticism.

Ten minutes later the old man began to stir. Sterling passed Penelope over the patient's body.

"Marked improvement," read the diagnosis. "Prescribe much fluid intake . . . nonalcoholic."

Arkassi craned his neck to read the digital message.

"*Gottam!*" he exclaimed. "That one helluva watch!" He went out the door.

The old man blinked his eyes and his mouth worked. Lafia put away her knife, fell to her

knees, and covered the old man's face and bald
head with grateful kisses.

Arkassi returned shortly with a pitcher.

"Fluid!" exclaimed Arkassi. "Water from snow
mixed with Rosamma elixir! Dust from strange
flower, Rosamma. Full of—how you call—vital, vital . . ."

"Vitamins," said Sterling.

"Tam right! Tam full of vitamins. Make strong
in few hours."

He handed the pitcher to Lafia, who propped
her father's head up and held a cup of the liquid to
his lips. He drank. Then he drank again. He smiled
weakly at his daughter and whispered the Russian
equivalent of cheers: "*Zha vashe zhdorovye!*"

So he *was* Russian, he was over one hundred
years old, and he had a story to tell. This must be
Alexandra's man.

Sterling started to ask him some questions, but
the man whispered, "Sleep . . ." and closed his
eyes. Lafia picked up the lantern, tucked the coverlet around her father, and stood up. She spoke
to Arkassi.

"She show us to our house," he said opening the
door. It was already dark out.

They followed her out the door toward the other
cottage. She and Arkassi talked in low voices in
their language as they walked ahead of Sterling.
When they entered the cottage, he saw that it was
like the other cottage except that here there were
more books and a crude wooden desk and two low

beds. Lafia put down the lamp and turned in the center of the room, gesturing first to herself and then to the house.

"It is all yours, sah," said Arkassi with a grin. "Especially her."

Sterling looked at him blankly.

"No understand?" asked Arkassi conspiratorially. "Is custom this part of world. You save chief's life, you take youngest daughter."

"You mean . . ."

"Means what you want. You take . . . you marry . . . you sleep with . . . what you want."

"But I really don't—"

"You lucky," said Arkassi, heading for the door, "Lafia over fifteen. I save chief's life once . . . his daughter only eleven!" His laugh boomed, and he called as he went out, "Sweet dreams, sah!"

"Wait," said Sterling. "Look, there's a bed for you here. Don't go!"

"I take care of old man, you take care of Lafia," and he was gone. When Sterling turned, he saw Lafia walking toward him, her black eyes burning. He backed up saying, "Hello, I must be going."

The knife was in her hand. She held it against his throat. With her left hand she undid the bone buttons of her deerskin jacket, exposing the fullness of the crimson blouse. Slowly she undid the buttons of the blouse. Her breasts, their pink nipples large and erect, forced aside the shirt and jacket. She took one of Sterling's hands and placed it on the tawny skin of one firm breast. Sterling sighed. "I wonder how one can ever explain this sort of thing to a girl like Melanie . . . ?"

Lafia looked at him quizzically. Melanie's face flashed briefly in front of him but he said nothing. And after gently pushing aside the knife blade with his forefinger, he leaned forward and kissed the luscious, half-parted lips.

How many hours later, he didn't know, Sterling heard a banging and stumbling at the door.

"You come, sah!"

It was Arkassi with a lantern who came crashing into the cottage. "Old man awake! Want to talk with you. Want *raki*, want food!"

Arkassi looked as though he'd had a good bit of *raki* himself, Sterling thought sleepily as he untangled himself from Lafia's beautiful body. He reached over, found Penelope, and put her on. Then he got out of bed and dressed himself. Lafia threw back the wool coverlet and, naked and unashamed, stood up and began to dress. Arkassi, clothed but equally unashamed, stared at her breasts and studied the round buttocks and V-shaped pelt like an anatomy major.

"Animal," she said matter-of-factly to Arkassi as she slipped on her leather jacket and picked up the lamp.

"A compliment, thank you." He nodded in agreement and followed her out the door.

"Sah, you like local custom now?" asked Arkassi

as they made their way in the dark night to the other cottage.

"I could grow fond of them," replied Sterling, gravely. "Very, very fond."

Inside the dwelling the old man was sitting up. His eyes were alert, black like his daughter's, and he looked as though he'd never been ill.

"*Raki*," he said to his daughter.

"Sir, *raki* made you ill," said Sterling in Russian. "Better wait awhile, a few weeks. The liver is a very forgiving organ, unlike the brain. Maybe in a few weeks you can drink *raki* again, in moderation."

The old man looked at Sterling with narrowed eyes and sniffed contemptuously. "You talk like Russian doctor."

"I am neither."

"I know."

"You know a great deal I think," said Sterling. "Did you know Alexandra Robinson? And why she was coming to see you?"

"I do not know that name."

A glance at Penelope showed green diodes as the old man spoke.

"But you know Natasha?"

"No," he answered, and the green diodes showed he was still telling the truth. "I have never met Natasha."

"But your daughter . . . she said . . ."

"Natasha is my great-granddaughter, but I have never seen her. I have never seen my grandson. I have been here for"—he waved his hand airily to indicate the many decades he had been here— "almost seventy-five years. But I know about my family, Serge and Boris and Anna and little Natasha . . . not so little now, must be thirty years old."

At first Sterling thought not to tell the old man about Natasha, not to cause him pain. But then he had been truthful with Sterling, so he told him about Alexandra and Marrakesh and Natasha's murder truthfully and completely.

The old man's eyes narrowed and he swayed back, but all he said was, "My poor Boris. And his wife. They will grieve."

They sat in silence for a moment. Then Sterling said quietly, "There are so many unanswered questions, sir. What do you make of all of it?"

The old man's lips moved wordlessly and then he said, "The curse of Tungusky . . . it still goes on. I cannot escape it, even here at the end of the world."

"I don't understand, sir."

"Tungusky . . . that is what killed poor Natasha. Seventy-three years later."

"Tungusky?"

"Surely you, whom I understand to be an extraordinarily intelligent man, have heard of that cataclysmic happening so long ago?"

Sterling had read books and scientific papers on the great riddle that had happened in Siberia in 1908. Thousands of terrified witnesses saw the horrendous explosion that June near the Tungusky River. Tens of thousands of trees were leveled. It was the greatest blast known to mankind, comparable to an H-bomb. Yet scientists could not explain it. It occurred high in the air in a nuclear fashion, leaving no craters on the ground and no recognizable traces. Weird scenarios of antimatter meteors, miniature black holes, lithium asteroids, fiery whirlwinds, ball lightning, and other exotic phenomena were suggested over the following years as an explanation. A favorite theory was that the explosion was caused by a collision of Earth with a small comet, probably a chunk off a dying space "snowball" named Encke's comet . . . yet how then the absence of a crater?

Suddenly, imperiously, the old man waved his daughter and Arkassi out of the room.

"They speculate it was a flying saucer that exploded," said Sterling.

The old man's eyes closed with mirth as he gave a wheezing breathy laugh. "Idiots! If a UFO . . . why was no iron or other metal found at the blast site?"

"Some say it was a nuclear blast sent by an alien force and set off to attract attention."

The old man's eyes twinkled in the lantern's light, "Ah, now you are coming closer to the truth. It *was* a nuclear blast, it *did* attract attention and"—he tapped his chest—"here is your alien force."

"You . . . you had something to do with Tungusky?"

"I am Tungusky."

"What, sir, if I may ask, is your name?"

"Reverof."

"Reverof." Sterling's mind worked quickly. And almost as quickly as the enigma was deciphered by Penelope, he was recalling the message Alexandra had left in Marrakesh: "On a new clear day you can see forever." On a nuclear day you can see Reverof.

"Reverof is a name I took when I first came here. My real name is Alexander Vasilief."

Sterling's mind raced frantically. Vasilief? It can't be, Sterling thought. Vasilief, the extraordinary Russian scientist of the beginning of the century, *still alive?*

"But," exclaimed Sterling, "I thought you were dead!"

The old man wheezed with laughter. "So did the world!" he finally aspirated, choking and coughing on his words. "The whole world thinks I am dead . . . to the world I *am* dead! Tungusky not only blasted away all the trees, it blasted *me* away also!"

Seeing the fascinated look on Sterling's face, he cocked his head slyly. "Interested, eh?"

Sterling nodded. "Interested and confused."

"Because you only have heard interesting and confusing reports . . . the real story no one has heard. You would be the first to hear it if I decide to tell you. But it is better that I tell someone, because it is not good that the world does not know what has happened at Tungusky. Natasha knew part of the story—passed down from her father, from her grandfather, from me. Some she must have told to your friend . . . what was her name?"

"Alexandra Robinson."

"This Alexandra Robinson wanted to come here to see Natasha's great-grandfather, eh? To find out what was the story of Tungusky, eh? I would not have told her. It is not a story for a woman to worry about. But I think I will tell you."

Sterling waited expectantly.

"*Ya hotchu pyet*," whispered the old man. "*Raki*."

Sterling hesitated. "Sir, your liver . . ."

"Show your respect with *raki*! It takes more than *raki*, but a little *raki* can sharpen my memory!"

Sterling glanced over at the bottles. "They are all empty."

"*Pleshkov's Theories*," he said.

Sterling didn't move.

The old man chuckled. "Look behind that big book . . . *Pleshkov's Theories*."

Sterling leaned over, pulled out the big volume, and took out the half-filled bottle. He poured a small amount into the cup by the man's pallet.

"One now," said Vasilief, "as a bribe and one after, as a reward."

He drank and then began to talk. He told Sterling of his early experiments in Moscow, radical experiments, the first ever with atomic reactors. But he could not go far with the restrictions imposed on him by the Russian government and the turmoil of the times. He withdrew from society to develop his theories. His great passion, his obsession, was to uncover the eternal secret of the origins of matter as an answer to so many forthcoming problems of the world. He wanted the answer to be an overwhelming argument for peace—a force so devastating that it would impose peace on a belligerent world.

His experiments, he knew, were closely watched by the government, so one day he and his older son fled to Siberia—to the Tungusky River region—with all their equipment and data. After several months they succeeded in designing and mounting a primitive proton accelerator that would prove his theories . . . or disprove them. He felt very close to the eternal secret.

Two total failures did not discourage him and then one June morning—a bitterly cold Siberian June day—he and his son activated the equipment again. The protons circled at tremendous speed around the short tunnel. But then his son, for some unfathomable reason, opened a hatch prematurely. The protons changed course, cold air blasted into the tunnel, the collision of protons melted the core of the tunnel and expanded into a cataclysmic explosion.

His son, in the eye of the blast, was vaporized immediately. Vasilief, a good distance away, was in the neutral crater section. Everything beyond the twenty meters around him was destroyed.

"My foolish experiment could have destroyed Russia, as it did my poor son. I took this, my salvation, as an omen. I knew then that I was close to something so big that if the government got it, they would use it to destroy the world. They believed me dead in the blast, and I obliged them by disappearing. After some incredible adventures I found my way here to paradise. I have been here ever since, unmolested . . . until just recently when my great-grandaughter Natasha alerted me to the fact that some American was on the way to see me. For Natasha to have told someone—anyone—of my whereabouts . . . it must have been of the utmost importance. Not to her, not to me," his strong old voice trembled, "but to the world."

"Your secret," said Sterling, "your deadly secret . . . what would happen if people now, so many years after your fatal experiment, knowing what we know now, the technology of today, what if they improved on your theory . . . took all the precautions that you didn't take?"

The old man smiled faintly and shook his head. "Today . . . hah! With the way science has to cover up all the lethal elements with the pretense of safety measures, hah! The world would be doomed."

"Supposing an experiment were to be mounted today just like yours in Tungusky, only on a much, much larger scale of acceleration, what then?"

"The earth would shrink around its core, become small like this." He held out his fist and shook it. "Small, small, small, like an apple, but a mighty ball of gravity, you understand? A black hole . . . you know what is a black hole? A very massive star collapsing, sucking everything into it, including light!"

Sterling drew in his breath. "I believe they are in the process of doing just that."

"Who is *they*?"

"The American government. With the best intentions in the world, we are about to do just that . . . destroy the world."

"More than that," said Vasilief, matter-of-factly. "Perhaps our universe."

"I still can't understand it fully," Sterling said. "Until now all experiments with matter and antimatter were successful."

"*Raki*," said the old man, pointing weakly toward his cup. "You promised."

Sterling gave him a sip.

"You can take the clay pot to the fountain many times," said the old man, licking his lips. "It only breaks once."

"Meaning?"

"Meaning that you can fool around with experiments of this sort as long as you are humble and you don't have visions of playing God. Meaning that when you are a termite, you can chew wood as long as you don't bring the whole house down on your tiny head. Young man . . . what is your name?"

"Sterling."

"Young man, Sterling, take a look around you. The universe is made out of tiny unseen molecules. Trillions of molecules form our very existence, and we are nothing but trillions of molecules, held together by some glue, right?"

Sterling nodded.

"Now, suppose you found a way to raise your little finger and make the glue disappear, then all the molecules would dance away, and you would be thin air before you even knew it."

"That's how the theory wants it. But . . . the end of the world because of an atom-collision experiment?"

Vasilief rested his head in his hands. "They are trying to find the origins of matter, aren't they?"

Sterling nodded silently.

Vasilief continued, "They are dreaming of discovering the beginning of life, the very core of creation. What they do not realize is that this universe is standing in front of a mirror. But we have been doing it for so long that we have lost the sensation of seeing things reversed, where the right is left and the left is right. We think that the mirror is the reality instead of the image . . ."

He paused, cleared his throat, and downed the *raki* in the cup. "What we are looking at, in this experiment, is not the beginning of our universe," he said hoarsely.

His deep, piercing eyes were burning as he said, "It is the end."

He raised a finger and pointed to the sky. "The glue that holds everything together has more than one ingredient. It is science and philosophy, and sometimes the two create a strange mixture that is called religion. We can only go that far in research and experimentation. There is always a limit and we cannot push it farther. The experiment of such a colossal magnitude will destroy the glue. And the mirror will break a tiny nano-second after we have realized that instead of throwing stones into the abyss, we were throwing stones at the glass partition that separated and protected us from the abyss."

Sterling felt cold and his heart was pumping hard. "What do you suggest?" he asked.

Vasilief chuckled and looked at the ceiling. "Forget about the origins of matter. Forget about the ultimate form of energy. Forget the greed. Everything has a beginning and an end. The world will start another cycle and it will survive, for as long as the glue holds together the zillions of molecules. Forget evolution. Forget improvement. Go back to the stone age, reinvent the wheel, rediscover fire. That will take you away from the mirror and then you can start throwing stones again."

CHAPTER THIRTEEN

The return trip from Gorak Shep to Gilgit was easier and faster than Sterling had expected. Arkassi brought their party back a day and a half after leaving Vasilief.

When Sterling said farewell to Arkassi, they shook hands warmly, for each had developed a true respect for the other's abilities.

Arkassi's eyes darkened as he said, "So, we don't see each other again."

Sterling nodded but replied, "This is an interesting part of the world, Arkassi. Perhaps, someday when I have free time, I might be back to let you show me more of it. I would insist on having 'the world's greates' guide'!"

Arkassi's face crinkled as he guffawed, "Tam right!"

Sterling chuckled when he gave one last wave to the huge man with the corrugated brown face still watching him as he turned into the hotel doorway.

Sterling hurried to the room where he'd left Melanie and tapped on the door. When he answered her "Who is it?" the door was flung open, and she threw her arms around him and buried her head against his chest. "You're all right! Oh, thank God, you're all right!"

He laughed softly and said in a mock-surprise tone, "I didn't know you cared!"

"Damn you! Of course I care! Who else do I know in this grubby little town on the edge of nowhere?"

Melanie then walked away from him, asking, "Did you strike oil in Gorak Shep?"

"You might say that," Sterling replied. "And if you like, I'll tell you about it while we eat something. This mountain air and exercise have given me an appetite."

Soon after he finished eating and while still talking to Melanie about his experiences in the mountains, Sterling brought out a large suitcase. Melanie watched in fascination as he removed from it colored wires, screws, coils, and transistors and various other components.

"So much for the Pierre Cardin and Guccis I thought were in here," she said as she watched him assemble a small color television monitor.

"If you're planning to catch the *Tonight* show, I

hear Carson's out of town," she said when he had finished.

"You know what this is?" he asked Melanie.

"Of course," she replied. "We are at last going to see Penelope's face." He was connecting the set to his wrist terminal with a line of fiber optics.

He switched the monitor on. "I am connecting this monitor to Penelope's visual-image synthesizer," he said. "We may be able to confirm Vasilief's theory."

"I wish I could have met him," said Melanie, suddenly serious. "Imagine a scientist like that, living in a place like this . . . and so old, so incredibly old."

"And wise. He thinks we're going to turn this planet into a tennis ball."

"That should make a lot of people in Beverly Hills happy," said Melanie.

Sterling spoke to his wrist terminal. "All right, sweetheart. You have the coordinates from the recorded conversation with Vasilief. You have my coordinates and Alfreds's schematics of the proton collision. I want you to compare our data with Vasilief's data and come up with a visual simulation of what's happening in this experiment."

Then he looked at Melanie. She put her hand on his.

Penelope came back with a question. "I am unable to combine data. Vasilief's theory contradicts the schematics from Professor Alfreds. Your suggestion."

"Go ahead and do it separately. Give us visuals on Alfreds's experiment first."

To their amazement the monitor came on with a dazzling display of the protons colliding. Using computer graphics and actual footage from Fermi Laboratories, Penelope produced the ultimate light show as the screen filled with violent colors, strange shapes, and multiple miniature explosions.

"This," Sterling said, "is the microphotography of a proton, stripped down to its origins. Alfreds is hoping to achieve the ultimate apocalypse—what matter is made from and how this universe started."

"I see no danger in it," Melanie said, shrugging.

"Only because Penelope simulated his theory. But Vasilief said we were looking into a mirror, and therefore the right seemed to us left and vice versa. If this is the case . . ."

Sterling punched several buttons. "Penelope, reverse all of Alfred's theory. Simulate as if everything was played in a mirror."

Penelope said she needed to reprogram the synthesizer and this would take some time.

As he paced up and down the room, waiting, he thought, Alfreds, the old goat, he was right! He was just a jump away from uncovering the Great Secret, the creation of life, the very beginning of the universe itself!

Then the disquieting afterthoughts: How close to God, and to playing God, should Man get? And how altruistic and genuine was Alfreds's interest in this new form of energy for mankind? Was he guided by personal ambitions and hunger for power, the temptations of so many modern scientists? Was he exploiting the young, ambitious President's desire for more political clout by promising him and the Russians this ultimate discovery: instant God?

He glanced at Melanie. After the mesmerizing show, doubts were clearly materializing, as evidenced by her troubled frown.

"What's the matter?"

"Nothing, really," Melanie said. "Except . . ."

"Except?"

"Well, of course, I don't know the first thing about all this. I barely understood what I was watching. But . . ."

"But?"

"But sometimes rank amateurs can see things better than professionals . . . or feel them."

"Really? Such as for instance?"

"Such as . . . Noah was an amateur . . . the *Titanic* was built by professionals. I just feel that what he saw was 'what-if-everything-goes-right.' All I'm saying is that it could be the biggest *Titanic* of all time. There just have to be some unknown factors . . . I don't care how brilliant Professor Alfreds and your Russian genius are. It seems to me that when people start messing around with Mother Nature the old girl often gets bitchy and rears back and really lets them have it!"

While he waited for the computer to come up with some alternative answers, he put a call in to Dr. Monroe at Mann Industries. When Monroe finally came to the phone, Sterling talked to him guardedly.

"What in the world are you up to, Sterling?" came the anxious familiar voice from so far away.

"Can't go into that now, Uncle Hank . . . just ship me Consignment Z here in Gilgit soonest. All's well and Melanie sends love."

"But, Sterling, hold on, Consignment Z is due for delivery to the Department of Defense in three days."

"So I'll have it back in three days," said Sterling succinctly.

"But, Sterling, we can't—"

"Yes, we can. Important, Uncle Hank!" Sterling said. "Very important. Can't talk . . . okay?"

A little while after he had returned to the room, the TV set crackled into life and on the screen appeared a series of formulae. Sterling crouched in front of the TV writing down the words and numbers rapidly. To Melanie they looked like hieroglyphics of some ancient culture, but Sterling kept saying, "Brilliant . . . brilliant!"

"And what does that mean for us dum-dums?"

"You were right. Penelope has discovered an unbalanced factor! It's in the cooling process in the tunnels and the length of the route that the protons must follow!"

Melanie had never seen Sterling so excited and

she murmured, "At last! Now that I know how to turn you on, I doubt I can ever do it again."

Sterling asked Penelope to show him exact lengths relative to exact temperatures, for the longer the tunnels, the colder the magnets had to be to sustain the tremendous heat generated by the acceleration. Penelope counted and measured, and it all seemed controllable until just before the proton collision.

"A definite danger exists when tunnels exceed sixty miles," the screen read.

"But that's impossible," said Sterling. "Where on earth could they find a sixty-mile tunnel?"

"Not on earth," replied Penelope.

Of course. He explained to Melanie that two years ago he had proposed to the government a space station that would carry linking equipment for laser beams interconnecting in space to link in freezing temperatures, and thus provide scientists with an uncommonly safe and controllable acceleration route. His ideas were met with resounding apathy, he thought, at the time. Yet now . . .

"Bastards!" he said. "Now they are doing it. Alfreds is doing it! And they're going to mess it up!"

"What will happen?" Melanie breathed.

Sterling shrugged. "Let's ask the Delphi oracle."

He asked Penelope to assign all the information on the experiment to her image synthesizer and to come up with a graphic picture of what would happen if the experiment were indeed accelerated to interconnecting laser beams that would extend to a space station.

In a few moments they were watching a series of pictures. In awe. First, the protons, starting from their ground station, sped up in five-mile-long tunnels in that station, and then when the acceleration reached a point of no gravitation, the protons were diverted into an "up" laser beam that took them seventy-two miles into space and then brought them back to earth at speeds, incredibly enough, even exceeding the speed of light.

After the frantic journey from the artificially cooled lab tunnels to the natural freezing temperatures of outer space, increasing in speed, gaining in power, then ultimately meeting head on with each other in a seemingly endless collision, slowed down by Penelope's image synthesizer to one to one million, the particles flew and danced and spun before their eyes like bouquets of multicolored flowers. Then the blinding light of a nuclear explosion burst from the core of the protons, releasing a series of multiplying explosions invisible to the naked eye, but very visible on the TV screen and horrendous in their devastation. In a chain reaction of collisions the surrounding area was consumed, the ground disintegrated, and in a minute a nebula developed—an uncontrollable stellar holocaust, with earth at the center.

"Oh, God!" Melanie breathed. "Look . . . dear God . . . look!"

The world was shriveling before their eyes, growing wrinkled and scorched as it shrunk and shrunk until finally it was the size, color, and texture of an orange. And then what had been the living earth became a death trap, sucking in its narrow abyss, like a voracious mouth, the neighboring planets, stars, the sun, the moon, and then the screen went dead.

They sat stunned. This educated guesswork, made only by a piece of machinery and computer-produced, had been frighteningly lifelike in its depiction of the ultimate tragedy—the total universal catastrophe.

"So?" Melanie, near tears, managed to say finally. "Now what?"

Sterling said nothing, only shaking his head in anger and frustration and staring out at the dark Himalayan night—a perfect portrait of a black hole.

They were both too drained and absorbed in their own thoughts to hear the sounds outside their window; four cars approached the back of the hotel and skidded to a stop. They were dark old cars, like most in Gilgit, but they were the best available and they were packed with armed men. The uniformed men scrambled out of the vehicles, weapons drawn, and gathered in the cobblestone courtyard whispering.

Normally Sterling's acute senses would have alerted him to the unusual sounds, but he was lost in what he had just seen on the screen. Dispiritedly, he began to dismantle the TV set and the image synthsizer and to disconnect them from Penelope, while Melanie paced.

"My head is splitting like those damned atoms," she said.

She took an aspirin from her purse. Warned not to drink the tap water, she went to Sterling's open knapsack and took out one of the Coke cans. She pulled the ring and the can hissed. And continued to hiss like a cobra.

Sterling, down on his knees working on the TV set, heard the noise. He whirled, leaped up, and snatched the can from her hand. Running to the window, he hurled it out into the darkness. The hissing can arched through the night air, bounced on the cobblestones, and then exploded with tremendous force. Four men fell to the ground, dead and torn; three others were badly wounded.

Sterling was appalled at the results until suddenly other uniformed men materialized and began firing at his window. He stepped back, and grabbing the knapsack, he said, "Let's get out of here."

He took Melanie by the hand and ran out into the corridor. It was dark, but with his incredibly keen eyesight he guided her swiftly down the steep stairs.

They came out into the lobby, and he saw that it was swarming with armed men. Stealthily, Sterling pressed himself against the wall and edged himself and Melanie toward an open side door.

Suddenly there was a shout as they were spotted, and several of the men raised their weapons. Sterling pushed Melanie through the doorway as the first shots rang out, and at the same time he spun and lobbed one of the Coke grenades into their midst.

The explosion lofted mangled bodies into the air, slammed tables and chairs against the walls, and caused the big brass chandelier to crash down on the screaming men, but Sterling didn't wait to examine the results. He grabbed Melanie's hand again and they sprinted toward the first car in the courtyard. The driver was half out the door and fumbling for his pistol when Sterling caught him flush on the jaw with a solid right. The man went down and Sterling dragged him to the side.

The old car came alive under Sterling's hands, and they sped down one dark alley after another.

In one hour they were safely out of the city in a primitive countryside, and no one was in pursuit. Sterling pulled off the dirt road into a clump of trees by a grassy meadow. They could see the dark shapes of sleeping yaks, like silhouettes of cave drawings of bison and aurochs. He put his arm around Melanie and sagged back in his seat with a sigh.

"Long day," said Melanie.

Sterling nodded in agreement, his eyes closed and frowning.

"Something's bothering you," she said.

234 NICO MASTORAKIS AND BARNABY CONRAD

"You mean, other than the bind we were just in and the prospect of blowing up the universe . . . little things like that?"

"Something else . . . something else is bugging you."

"Someone has been tipping off the enemy," he said flatly. "Wrong, not the enemy, the misguided good guys."

"Why? How can you tell?"

"All my moves . . . they know my every movement. So who is it? Only a few qualify for finkdom. Nicholas?"

"Never. He's been with you forever. He'd never be a fink. He adores you!"

"Uncle Hank?"

"Out of the question, and you know it."

"You're right. Nicholas knew sometimes where I was going but not always. Even Uncle Hank didn't know everything. But one person was fully informed, someone I trusted blindly, even though it was against my normal and natural instincts to trust her without checking her out thoroughly first."

"Her?" repeated Melanie.

"She could have been planted on me from the beginning." His eyes burned as he looked at her. "She could just have happened to be hitchhiking on a certain day when . . ."

"You surely don't mean . . ."

"Yes, Melanie, reluctantly I do. You could always provide the project's security people with my itinerary, my thoughts, my progress in the investigation. You, my sweet Melanie Ross, are the fink."

As he said these last words he picked up the remaining Coke can. Melanie's eyes widened in terror.

"Crazy!" she breathed. "You are crazy!"

He lifted the ring on top of the can. When it hissed, she pushed open the door and started running across the meadow toward a grove of trees.

Sterling watched her go for a moment, then raised the can to his lips and took a sip. Then he said to his watch, "The girl is dead, Penelope."

"Yes, sir."

"I am going to get some sleep, sweetheart," he said. "And I want you to go to sleep for a while also. I wish you a good seven-forty-eight."

"Seventy-forty-eight?"

"Yes."

Penelope quickly scanned her memory banks for the code number, then obeyed as directed and disconnected herself from Sterling. As she did, Sterling once more entered the quiet world of the deaf, not a pleasant but a familiar world that held no terrors for him. He got out of the car and walked out across the meadow in the moonlight toward the trees, calling Melanie's name.

"Come out, darling," he said. "Look . . . nothing to fear. I'm sorry."

He drank from the can, then poured the rest slowly out as he walked. Finally, still trembling with fear, Melanie emerged from the copse. Then anger replaced her fear.

"What the hell was that all about, Sterling!"

He could barely read her lips in the pale moonlight.

Sterling explained how he had indeed thought for a while that Melanie might have been the traitor. But she did not know any of the details of the Marrakesh trip and also—an important fact—she had been exposed to danger while with him.

"No, there is only one who has always known my whereabouts and plans." He pointed at the wrist terminal. "Penelope."

Melanie said in amazement, "She . . . she is the traitor?"

He could tell by her expression that she was whispering.

"You don't have to whisper . . . she can't hear now. And no, she's not a traitor. There is no traitor. The so-called enemy—our own government—owns the satellite that I use to transmit Penelope. Somewhere along the line the 'enemy' found out the channel I kept exclusively for myself and I was monitored. When Alexandra called me with the news that she'd discovered something of vast importance, the call was received by Penelope . . . and was monitored. They kept monitoring me, waiting . . . waiting. Of course they know all about Reverof, too, and that I know about the experiment. That's why they decided to attack tonight, a drastic move because they felt the situa-

tion had gotten out of hand. No more riddles
. . . just facts. I've got them and they know it."

"So, what about Penelope?"

He strained to read her lips. "What?"

"Penelope."

"I just ordered her to seven-forty-eight . . . to
commit suicide as it were. I'll connect her when I
get back to New York. Meanwhile, she's deaf.
And . . ." He struggled for words. "Melanie
. . . I . . ."

She had never seen him at a loss for anything,
much less words. "Yes, Sterling . . . what? What
is it?"

"So am I!"

"What do you mean?" Melanie looked at him,
confused.

"I am deaf, too!" Sterling reinforced the statement by signing. "I was born deaf. I depend upon
Penelope to augment my defective frequencies."

"Oh, Sterling, darling!"

He led her to a large tree and they sat down at
the base of it. He then told her about his early
years, his affliction, and the development of Penelope.

"You're human," she signed, eyes filled with
tears. "You're human . . . you have a flaw!"

"Not only human," Sterling said as he kissed her
tenderly. "But vulnerable. I need you. Tomorrow
I have Consignment Z coming in to the airport. I
need you to be my ears."

"Consignment Z?"

"An airplane. Equipped with all manner of sophisticated detection devices . . . a flying lab . . ." He looked at her for a long moment. "If you want to catch a plane out of here, I'll understand. This will be dangerous."

She shook her head. "Would Nancy Drew quit at a time like this? I'll go with you anywhere . . . to the end of the earth," she signed.

"That's a distinct possibility," he said as he wrapped a paper-thin thermo-electric blanket around the two of them and they settled back to sleep the rest of the night.

High noon and the small airport on the outside of Gilgit was quiet. The only activity was centered around a military weapons carrier that was parked near the runway. Sterling and Melanie were hidden in the bushes at the end of the runway, waiting for Consignment Z. They waited and waited.

The soldiers appeared to be waiting for something too. Clearly they were stationed at the airport to intercept Sterling and Melanie should they try to leave Gilgit by plane. Other units were stationed at the various possible points of departure, all alert for signs of Sterling.

The group of soldiers by the weapons carrier squatted in the sun, smoking, chatting, their rifles slung across their backs, throwing a stick for a large, woolly Bantu puppy. They threw the stick farther and farther each time and the dog joyously retrieved it. The last time the stick landed a few feet from the bushes where Melanie and Sterling were hiding, and when the dog bounded up and took the stick in his mouth, they could have stroked his brown wool. The big puppy looked right at them, wagged his tail happily, and romped back to the soldiers with his prize.

Sterling took the ground-to-air radio from his knapsack and pulled out the telescopic aerial. The small unit had no trouble reaching the pilot of Consignment Z. He held the instrument to Melanie's mouth.

"Ask for Mr. Slater . . . find out his position and ETA."

Melanie did, and amid a crackling of static a man's voice replied, "Who the hell are you? I take orders only from the boss."

Melanie relayed the message to Sterling, and he spoke into the radio: "It's okay, Ed, she's with me. Where are you?"

"About sixteen miles south of you . . . be there pronto. Goddamn, some flat land's gonna look damn good after all these mountains."

Melanie signed the message to Sterling.

"Okay, Ed, now you've got a really short operation here so hit the chute quick, then turn and get ready for a fast getaway."

"Sounds like good ol' Nam."

Sterling put the radio back in the knapsack and took out a device that looked like an extra-thick ruler, twelve inches long and one inch thick.

In a few minutes they spotted the small silhouette of Consignment Z coming in over the snow-covered mountains. It was a Boeing 749 painted jet black and with no writing or insignia on its fuselage.

At the same time one of the soldiers arced the stick through the air, and it landed very close to Sterling's hiding place again. Quickly he took his rulerlike instrument and twisted the end section clockwise one turn. A tiny red diode came on. He stealthily reached out from the bushes and grabbed the dog's stick. When the animal came bouncing up, Sterling tossed out his device. Happy with the new toy, the dog snapped it up in his mouth and ran back across the runway to the soldiers. But they were now engrossed in watching the approaching plane as it dropped its nose and began floating down toward a landing as though in slow motion.

"When I say 'run,'" said Sterling as he put on his knapsack, "do the same like crazy."

The dog barked for someone to throw his new toy for him, wagging his tail and cocking his head in silent appeal. The little red light was blinking now on the ground in front of the puppy. The soldiers were not paying attention; they were too busy watching the 749 as its wheels touched the runway and a huge parachute blossomed out behind its tail.

Sterling stood up and hurled the stick that the dog had left across the field but away from the device with its blinking light. The dog sped happily for the new target.

"Now!" Sterling commanded, taking Melanie by the wrist. "Run!"

They came out of the bushes at a run, heading for the taxiing plane. The soldiers saw them now and raised their rifles and shouted. Sterling and Melanie ducked their heads and zigzagged toward the jet. It was slowing down but the runway was coming to an end . . . and a cliff . . . dangerously soon.

The red light on the device suddenly went out, followed by a blinding light and a great explosion. The cluster of soldiers were hurled into the air and came down mangled or dead. The weapons carrier turned into a fireball.

The huge tires on the jet screamed as the plane finally came to a halt, rocked forward, then spun in a tight turn, kicking up dust and pebbles. A door opened on the side of the big craft and a long metal ladder dropped down.

"Run, Melanie, run!" Sterling urged.

They had only thirty yards to go . . . then twenty . . . then . . .

A truck was driving fast toward them with three men in it, one driving, two manning the large machine gun mounted in the back. Fifty yards from the plane the driver spun the vehicle around and stopped and the gun began firing at Melanie and Sterling as they ran.

"Oh, God!" Melanie cried as a stuttering burst

of bullets stitched a seam in the asphalt a yard
from her feet.

They reached the ladder and Sterling boosted
her onto the lower rungs and she started scram-
bling up the long haul to the hatch. Sterling
turned toward the machine-gun fire before following her up the ladder. They were sitting ducks
and surely would be killed before they could get
inside the plane.

And then he saw him . . . behind the truck a
giant figure appeared from the trees, bursting out
from the branches like some mythological forest
god. He charged the truck with his climbing staff
cocked like a batter waiting for a fast ball.

"Arkassi!" Sterling breathed as he climbed the
ladder behind Melanie.

Arkassi's first blow caught the gunner on the
side of the head and toppled him back out of the
vehicle, and the backhand of the same swing came
back to catch the cartridge belt feeder in the face.
Arkassi then jumped in the front, lifted the driver
from his seat as though he were a small sack of
fertilizer, and tossed him out onto the asphalt. He
waved jubilantly to Sterling, and roaring with
laughter like a child who has done a very clever
thing, he spun the vehicle around and sped from
the runway.

Waving back, Sterling went through the hatch,
slammed it behind him, sprinted up the long aisle
to the cockpit, and burst in.

"Great work, Slater!" panted Sterling as he buckled his seat belt. "Let's roll!"

The silver-haired man, no bigger than a jockey and with a large unlit cigar protruding from his mouth, had moved to the copilot's seat, and he grinned as his fingers touched the myriad knobs and levers as lyrically as a conductor leading an orchestra.

"We try to please, boss."

Reading Slater's lips as he put his hand on the throttle, Sterling asked, "Wife had the baby?"

"Twins, how about that?"

"Congratulations, you old devil!"

"Yeah, and we only did it once." He guffawed and chewed on his cigar as the plane began to move.

Melanie came in and dropped limply into the engineer's seat, saying weakly, "Coffee, tea, or Perrier," as Sterling shoved the throttles all the way forward and the big craft rolled down the runway. At the end of the asphalt ribbon Sterling could see some trucks and Jeeps lining up to shorten the runway to stop the plane's takeoff. The plane rolled faster and faster, straight toward them.

"Come on, baby!" Sterling urged, pushing on the throttles although they were as forward as possible.

"Go, darlin', go!" yelled Slater over the roar of the engines.

Even though the soldiers were now firing a variety of weapons at the oncoming plane, Sterling didn't dare attempt a lift off. But at the last moment, even though his ground speedometer indicated a normal takeoff speed had not been attained and a frantic red light flashed on and a warning horn sounded, Sterling eased back on the wheel.

The vehicles were only a few yards in front of the plane when the nose of the aircraft came up, and the soldiers cursed and dived for safety as the great shadow of the behemoth passed over them, its giant metal belly skimming the top of the vehicles precariously.

"Made it, boss!" exulted Slater.

As they climbed fast, Sterling glanced down out of the window looking for Arkassi. Sure enough, going fast on a dirt road, one could see the military vehicle kicking up dust, with its lone occupant. Sterling banked, flew over the truck, and wagged his wings in a last "thank you."

"Miss Ross," said Sterling, "you may tell the passengers the seat-belt sign is off and they are free to move about the cabin now."

He looked back to see Melanie deep in the first untroubled sleep in many days.

CHAPTER FOURTEEN

The control room was far below the ice of the Antarctic, the hub of the multibillion-dollar laboratory that buzzed with life. Its five-mile-long tunnels were as busy as an ant hill, with uniformed guards constantly patrolling and white-coated scientists in electric cars going to and fro in the corridors.

Alfreds kept glancing at the big digital clock on the wall, scratching his beard nervously as he did. He barked instructions to one man about the freon gas, which would be isolating and freezing the pipes in the tunnels. Then he ordered the video-tapes with the final secret instructions to be played over the hundreds of TV stations throughout the compound. The screens told the scientists and technicians that it was zero minus three hours now . . . the United States communications satellite Matchbox that would interlock two giant laser beams in space and complete the circuit for the acceleration of the protons would be in orbit in exactly two hours and forty-three minutes. It would take the laser beams less than one minute to connect with the satellite's internal sensor. From that moment on the entire lab would be on red alert. With the laser beams forming an arc from the earth to space, and with the protons already in acceleration in the tunnels, the experiment would be at its most crucial stage. The protons would attain the speed of light as they went from earth to space and back again to earth.

The exact moment of the head-on collision would be selected by the lab's giant computer, the protons being switched to a common channel.

The message concluded with Alfreds's voice saying solemnly, "And then, gentlemen, science will have the ultimate clues to the origins of matter, the beginning of time, the revelation of the perfect form of energy. The implications of this collision will be recorded by a brain that is almost human." On the screen came a picture of a chimpanzee—Greystoke—who was being fitted into a little astronaut suit.

"This uniform will protect him from the frighteningly cold temperatures that precede the experiment. As you can see, the helmet is wired with dozens of electrodes that will record for the computer bank a million vital readouts about the explosion. Regrettably the animal will die, but not before immeasurably helping the world of science."

Greystoke looked mournfully at the TV camera as though he knew what his fate was to be.

Now as Alfreds's skilled fingers pushed buttons, the TV monitors skipped around checking the various activities of the huge plant under Alfreds's critical scrutiny. The assistants, five male and one female, made quiet comments as the images flashed on the screen.

There was the giant generator that produced sixty times more electricity than was required by New York City, its power the essential drive of the two laser beams. The laser beam reflectors were ready on their swiveling bases to thrust energy out from the ice and aim at the satellite. Their targeting would be operated by the sophisticated unique computer that monitored Matchbox in space, and the same computer would make adjustments and compensations in following the movement of the satellite while the experiment was in progress.

The TV cameras now scanned the freon nozzles, huge phalluses that thrust out every ten feet along the cylindrical tunnels. Vital, totally vital to the experiment—the freon gas, plus the sine qua non, the ice of the Antarctic, would see that the temperature of the accelerating protons did not get out of hand and melt everything, granite, soil, metal, faster than the nuclear core in a China syndrome.

Now the TV cameras showed the submarine station and emergency port under the ice. Five small atomic submarines lay in the blue light guarded by their crews.

Another punch by Alfreds's finger and the TV screen showed a giant hangar with more than twenty armed Hovercrafts at the ready.

Next the helicopter platform: Three large helicopters, attached to each other by girders, warmed up—the whack-whack-whack of their motors making a deafening noise.

Finally Alfreds looked around the control room at his assistants.

"Well, lady and gentlemen," he said with a forced smile and an attempt at calm charm. "What do you say?"

The others nodded solemnly with comments like, "Seems all right," and "Everything is green, sir."

"All right then," said Alfreds, grimly now as he looked at the digital readout of the computer's timer. "Three hours minus six minutes."

His hands were so moist that tiny beads of perspiration glistened on the fingers, clinging to the fine hairs of the proximal phalanges of his hand.

On board the black 749 Melanie looked at Sterling quizzically as he flew the huge craft with obvious enjoyment. Slater was dozing after his long flight.

Sterling turned and was amused by her expression.

"You're wondering all sorts of things," he said. "Like why this big plane, where we're going, how we're going to find Alfreds before he blows up the world, and . . ."

She interrupted him, signing, "I have long since ceased to wonder anything about you, Sterling."

He gave a quiet little chuckle as he continued, "Well, it's just a reconnaissance flight over the area where I'm pretty sure Alfreds has set up his lethal little shop. It could be dangerous, so I'm going to peel off in a few minutes and Slater will fly you back to the States."

Melanie replied hotly, "No way, sir! I'm going with you!"

"Melanie . . . it could be plenty hairy!"

"I'm going with you, period! Remember, you need me . . . there's no Miss Penelope now."

Sterling reflected a moment. "That's true," he admitted. "All right, come on."

He shook Slater awake.

"See you back in the States, Ed."

The man took the controls, saying, "Take it careful, Sterling."

Sterling and Melanie left the cabin and walked into what would have been the first-class section had this been a commercial plane. The area was decorated in red, and out of a large closet Sterling took two red jump suits. He helped Melanie zip hers on, then quickly got into his.

He walked toward the tail of the plane through another area that was painted a metallic green, and the jump suits turned that color. As they stepped into a two-man elevator in the center of the airplane, the suits turned blue.

"At Mann Industries we call this material 'Chameleo,' " he said as he pressed the down button. "It's thermo-electric . . . takes on the exact color of its environment in two seconds."

When the elevator came to a stop, the doors opened and they stepped out into the dark belly of the gigantic airplane. Immediately their suits responded to the light condition and began to glow; by the light Sterling found a switch, pressed it, and a bright bluish light came on, revealing the precious cargo of the 749. Melanie was startled to see a snow-white, sleek two-seater jet hung from suspension coils in the bowels of the mother ship.

Sterling walked across a metal ramp and gestured for Melanie to get into the copilot's seat. Then he stepped in and strapped them both in.

Sterling flipped one switch, and a red digital readout began the countdown across the control panel. When it said TIME, Sterling's fingers went into action, darting from one switch and dial to another.

Suddenly the mother ship made a low purring sound, and the great underbelly split open slowly. Then the suspension coils freed the white jet from their embrace, and smoothly the small plane dropped down, engines alive, floating out and clear and away like a baby shark being born from its huge parent.

The engines kicked on. They saw the bay doors of the mother ship close again, and they watched it bank majestically to the west toward New York.

Melanie looked down. White . . . the incredible far reaches of snow, some of the thousands of miles of frozen water of the Antarctic stretched beneath her, five and a half-million square miles, ninety percent of the world's ice and snow.

"They're down there," Sterling mused. "They're all down there under the ice and busy as hell, you can bet."

"But how can you be so sure?" asked Melanie. "How do we know that? How do we know where?"

Sterling didn't answer, but turned on the three TV monitors. Then he pointed to the screens, which merely showed the vast expanse of ice below.

"Infrared aerial cameras . . . scanning from three different angles with three different magnification ratios . . . constantly sweeping . . . great scope. Anything camouflaged or hidden under the ice will show up—the infrared will pick up the heat emitted by whatever's down there."

"What makes you so sure anything *is* down there?"

"Process of elimination. Penelope told us that the experiment required freezing temperatures. Siberia? Russia? Out of the question. That leaves the Arctic and Antarctica . . . I instinctively feel it's here in the Antarctic; it's not populated."

"But Sterling . . ." She looked down through the windshield. "It's so enormous! Surely you can't expect to cover the whole Antarctic."

"It's not that haphazard. I've done some figuring as to where I'd go if I were Alfreds and wanted to put a gigantic installation in the Antarctic. He couldn't go just anywhere. I could be wrong . . . but it's an educated guess: Enderby Land, the closest point to Australia."

Melanie yawned and curled up in the seat.

"Your guesses are always educated. Wake me up if you see an Eskimo."

"Wrong end of the earth, darling," he said, patting her leg. "No Eskimos. But go to sleep and I'll wake you up if I spot Armageddon."

Many hours later Sterling's plane was detected in the radar room of the complex under the ice. The information was immediately given to the security officer, who picked up his direct phone to Dr. Alfreds.

"Professor, intruder plane spotted . . . unidentified, coming in from northwest . . . fast."

"Goddamn Arabs," he muttered. "Keep me posted . . . get ready to intercept it."

He quickly checked over his various instruments and computer readings as though to speed up the final phase, spurred on by the presence of the alien plane.

And already, on platform C of the Antarctic headquarters, three black, awesomely sleek jet fighters armed with air-to-air missiles were being slanted upward on hydraulic launchers for vertical takeoff.

High above the laboratory, Sterling saw something on one of the screens that caused him to point the nose of the jet down into a plummeting dive. He pulled out of the dive and slowed down as the cameras began showing clear infrared images of the gigantic installations beneath the ice.

"Melanie, look at the screens!"

"Lord, Sterling . . . you were right!"

The inbuilt computer interpreted the images as they were scanned: The entire installation was seven miles long by six miles wide, six hundred feet under the ice, and its nuclear core seemed the biggest that Sterling had ever heard of. It was ringed by ice mountains, as though nestled in a long-extinct volcanic crater.

"We'll make one more pass and then I'll take you home, young lady."

At that moment Sterling saw on the radar screen three shadows growing bigger and bigger. And then he glanced behind him and actually saw the black jet fighters pursuing him.

He shoved in the throttles and the jet leaped forward to full acceleration. Melanie, slammed back in the seat by the sudden speed, closed her eyes and murmured a prayer.

The on-board computer told Sterling the type

of aircraft, their top speed, and the fact that they carried air-to-air heat-guided missiles.

And then a very strange thing: Sterling suddenly could hear the roar of his own plane! And even hear Melanie's prayers! Her whispered prayers!

And Penelope, yes, the late Penelope, was saying, "Sterling, you can beat them. It's a tough job, but you can beat them!"

"I thought I told you to go to sleep!" Sterling exclaimed, trying to sound cross.

"I took a nap," Penelope replied. "But I had an awful dream that upset my circuits."

Sterling realized then that Penelope had interpreted his order correctly; she didn't completely disengage herself from transmitting and receiving, she had simply stayed mute to cut all bridges with the "enemy" while Sterling was trying to avoid detection. By intercepting the satellite from which Penelope and Sterling bounced their communications, the "enemy" was able to track Sterling. There could be no interception without transmission. Now that the enemy was already on Sterling's tail and he was in danger, Penelope's logic sensors reconnected her automatically with Sterling.

He was busy watching the black F-5E fighters as they were gaining on him when both Melanie and Penelope asked, "What are you going to do?"

"This!" said Sterling.

He shoved the controls forward and put the jet

into a screaming dive. Five hundred feet from the
ice, he pulled up, leveling off at a scant hundred
feet.

"Now we'll just circle the lab nice and low like
this . . . they'll never fire so close to their precious installation."

He was right, for the squadron leader of the
three fighters barked into his radio to the two others: "Ground security says to hold fire till he's out
of range!"

But they pursued and gained fast as they followed Sterling. When they came too close, Sterling suddenly pulled back on the controls, shot
straight up into the air, and let the black fighters
go underneath while he barrel rolled and then
came back behind them.

"The Lafayette Escadrille lives!" shouted Ster-
lind happily.

Dr. Alfreds, watching the radar screen, said between clenched teeth to his operations officer,
"Tell your men to be careful. We are dealing with
some suicidal mercenary . . . probably a crazy
Arab; he may crash us to try to set the whole goddamn thing off!"

The time scan on his screen showed that the
time for stage two was closing in. Nervously
Alfreds gave the prescribed commands and the
operators on the complex control panels pressed
the keys of the computer. And far above them, far
above the Antarctic in the vast silence of space,
the orbiting communications satellite, Matchbox I,

responded to the coded signals by coming to life. Its dark panels now awakened with flickering lights, more and more lights . . . and then clunkings, buzzings, hissing hydraulics, and the slow swiveling of two large reflectors. The gate to the laser beams had opened.

Sterling soon realized that his aerial musical chairs with the three fighters could not go on indefinitely. After the third zigzagging trip around the perimeter of the installation, he spotted a curious opening in the center of a crevice that ran down the ice mountain ahead. About fifty feet wide and two hundred feet high, it appeared to be the entrance to a natural tunnel.

"How long is it?" he asked Penelope.

"Two miles, four hundred feet," came the reply.

"Is there an opening at the end?"

"Curious you should ask," Penelope relied. "I can't determine that fact as there appears to be a bend in the middle."

"We'll take a chance."

Sterling throttled back and headed straight for the mouth of the tunnel.

"Oh, Lord, Sterling," Melanie breathed. "The wings are too wide for that opening!"

At the same time Penelope was warning, "Negative, Sterling, withdraw from action, negative . . ."

"Look out!" screamed Melanie.

But Sterling kept heading for the mountain, even as he heard the squadron leader's voice on the radio say, "Don't do anything, boys . . . the sonofabitch is gonna kill hisself for us!"

Closer and closer the white jet came to the hole, and it was obvious that the wings were much too wide to enter.

"Watch what the fucker's gonna do . . . same thing as before . . . pull straight up into a loop and try to get behind us. Let him have the machine guns when he barrel rolls!"

But Sterling didn't pull up, and he didn't slow down as the mountain loomed in front of him. One hundred feet from the mountain, he shoved the stick hard to the right, hit the aileron pedals, and with the wings vertical he entered the mouth of the tunnel.

The lead pursuing plane was caught unawares and frantically tried to bank away from the mountain. But his speed was too great, and the black jet crashed into the wall of ice and exploded. In desperation the two other fighters pulled straight up, did a wingover, and saved themselves.

"Goddamn, he got Charlie!" said the squadron leader as he circled. "Well, let's see how he likes fire up his ass . . . follow me in, Anderson, and drop both your Eagles!"

The leader banked sharply and headed back toward the mountain. Aiming his plane at the tunnel opening, he fired his two Eagle missiles, two long, heat-seeking tubes of death, and veered away. Behind him the second plane did the same.

"That'll fix his wagon!"

Inside the tunnel it was pitch black, and Sterling, still vertical, was flying on instruments—the plane's and Penelope's.

To complicate the predicament, Penelope said suddenly, "Heat-to-heat missiles directly behind you!"

At that instant there was a light at the end of the tunnel.

"Thank God for large favors!"

Sterling shoved the throttles all the way in. Shifting to supersonic speed, hitting Mach 1, caused a sonic boom behind his plane. Great chunks of ice in the tunnel walls vibrated and fell, taking two of the whistling Eagle missiles with them. But the other two made it through and Sterling could see them gaining on him, slithering like sharp-nosed cobras.

"Jam their frequency!" he said to Penelope urgently. "Jam it quick or you'll be an orphan!"

The gaping end of the tunnel was coming up fast, but so were the missiles.

"Come on, come on! Find the frequency . . . jam them!" Sterling urged, looking over his shoulder while still having to execute the intricate vertical flying maneuvers through the tunnel.

Penelope activated the jamming device, and the missiles wobbled and slowed momentarily. Sterling's plane shot out of the tunnel into the clear Antarctic sky, and he rolled it back over to a level position.

Melanie gasped, "And you're looking at the girl who hated roller coasters the most in the whole damn school!"

"Good boy, Sterling," said Penelope. "But look up!"

Sterling saw the two F-5E fighters up above him. They had flown over the mountain and the tunnel. They dropped immediately so that they were on his tail, and he heard the staccato of machine-gun bullets as he began to zigzag.

But he needn't have worried because, at that same moment, the two Eagle missiles, now unjammed, burst from the end of the tunnel and sped to the nearest objects giving off heat, which happened to be the engines of the two black fighters. They were suddenly transformed into blending fireballs in the crisp, frigid sky.

"Got any more tricks?" asked Melanie. "I could use a double martini about now."

Sterling squeezed her leg and said, "Sorry about this whole thing, darling. Just one more trick."

He pulled back on the stick and they shot almost straight up. Up, up, up, until he reached a point in the blue-black atmosphere beyond the reach of the installation's radar, then he eased the plane into a horizontal position and slowed it down.

"I'm sorry about all that down there," Sterling said. He took a handkerchief from his pocket and dabbed gently at her damp forehead. "I'd have left you behind if I'd known how close it would be."

Melanie kissed the back of his hand and murmured, "We all need a little adventure in our lives, I guess. And anyway, I asked for it, remember?"

"Brave girl," he said and kissed her.

"We're going back now?"

"We're going *down* now."

He reached behind the seat and wrestled out a parachute.

"One needs one," he said. "Actually, it's a sine qua non."

"Whatever that means."

"It means it is most advisable to wear one."

"Well, that makes more sense than 'without which not,' " she said as he helped her into it. "But did Caesar advise parachutes?"

From his inner pocket Sterling produced a pill box, gave her a red and white capsule and swallowed one himself.

"Romeo and Juliet at the South Pole?" she asked.

He didn't answer but dragged an oxygen mask from behind the seat.

"Anything to shut me up," she muttered as he strapped it on her head over her helmet.

Then he donned his own parachute and mask and said with a sigh, "Say good-bye to a ten-million-dollar beauty." He reached forward to the instrument panel and flipped a red switch.

Two rapid blasts followed and the jet shook violently. Melanie gasped as the two huge engines were blasted away from the plane. Then the entire fuselage began to shiver and vibrate. One mighty convulsion and the body of the plane cracked open. The two halves plus the split wings started the long spinning drop to the ground.

What was left was a light undetectable capsule built for two. It also began to descend, silently, as Sterling worked the few controls to keep it from tumbling. Down, down it went . . . now the altimeter read four thousand feet and still they dropped. Melanie found it strangely calm and peaceful.

"What about their radar?" she asked.

"That's the point of this," he replied.

At that very moment in the lab the operations officer was reporting, "The radar has picked up their debris, sir.

Alfreds looked pleased. "Good, good."

"Obviously the plane was damaged during the dogfight and exploded minutes later as they were trying to make their escape . . . probably heading for Australia."

"Fine, fine," Alfreds said. He didn't like or condone violence, but this experiment could brook no interference, no matter what the cost in human lives. "Any survivors?" he asked.

"None that we know of, sir. The radar hasn't picked up anything. They were too high to use 'chutes."

"Make sure . . . send out a patrol," said

Alfreds, going back to his controls. "Meanwhile, everyone, prepare for . . ." He hesitated at the enormity of it. "Get ready for stage three."

Meanwhile Sterling had leveled off the strange bubble at three thousand feet.

"Hold on to me," he said tersely, putting out his right hand. "And hold tight."

She took his hand and mumbled to keep her teeth from chattering too noticeably. "Have I mentioned that I suffer from high anxiety?"

Sterling flipped the eject lever, the canopy blew off, and both seats were catapulted into the air. With them went two bags of equipment.

At first it was a nightmare against which Melanie shut her eyes. Then the unique sensation of the free-fall became a pleasant dream, and she opened them again. Below her the vast frozen plateau was quickly coming up at them. Finally their chutes opened and the ones on the equipment packs blossomed as well.

"Don't worry," he shouted as they floated down and down. "The 'chutes . . . everything is painted with antiradar dye, an absorbent that makes us invisible to them down there."

He checked his bearings with Penelope.

"The lab is less than six miles away, northeast."

"Pretty accurate, sweetheart," he said with a chuckle. " 'Bout time you did something right."

Penelope's answering static bordered on being a rude sound.

* * *

At platform epsilon, under a vertical tunnel, three huge helicopters were preparing to launch the lift system. Attached to each other by metal girders, their great blades were already whirling when three Hovercrafts arrived full of uniformed personnel, some of them heavily armed.

The officer in charge shouted over his bullhorn: "At the surface craft one will search for any survivors of the destroyed jet . . . engineers and airlift personnel will proceed with assigned duties as planned."

He flashed a green light. Majestically the great helicopters rose and hung suspended twenty feet in the air. Quickly and efficiently people moved under the bellies of the aircraft to attach their hanging chains to the clamps on the sides of the Hovercraft. Then at a signal the trio rose as one, lifting their three siblings up the shaft as smoothly as an elevator.

Not far from the laboratory Sterling knelt on the ice in front of Melanie. In his hand was the low-helium laser pen. Unlike the delicate surgical instrument it had been with the old Russian, it was now turned up full beam and was performing like a powerful tool as he carved a hole in the ice four feet across and four to five feet deep. Sterling worked like a sculptor with soft plasticene as Melanie watched.

"That, I take it, is for litterbugs," kidded Melanie.

"Wrong." Sterling smiled as he continued to

smooth the surfaces. "It's where you are going to stay till I get back."

"Sterling!" she wailed. "You're joking!"

"Get in," he commanded. "See, I even carved a little seat for you . . . it will be your home away from home."

"I want to go with you!"

"Look, Melanie, I simply can't bear to expose you to any more danger than I already have. You mean too much to me, and the only comfort I could have at this point would be knowing that you do have a chance for survival this way. Please trust me, Melanie."

Melanie looked at him for a moment, then looked down.

Sterling went on, "Now I want you to keep your eyes on this and follow my instructions, okay?"

He dragged over the larger package that had been parachuted down with them. He stripped off the white cloth antiradar cover and revealed a five foot by four foot green object that looked like no more than a great garbage bag. On top was fastened an unlit light.

"When you see this light blink red, get ready. When it goes green, get into the yellow area."

"I don't see any yellow area."

"You will," he assured her. "Remember, when it goes green, think yellow."

"Sterling, I *am* yellow! Please don't leave me here. I don't want to play Nanook of the frozen South . . . I'll freeze!"

"No, you won't . . . the pill you took will keep you warm for twenty-four hours."

"And then?"

Sterling was packing some things in his knapsack from the parachuted supply package. "Then we're either home free . . ." He hesitated. "Or . . ."

"Or?"

"Or there will be no home anymore." He took out a small pistol and gave it to her.

"What about you?"

"I have this." He patted a weapon at his waist. "Don't worry about a thing," he said as he kissed her.

He put on a pair of adjustable skis. The surface here was not quite slick, perfect ice, nor was it completely snow-covered, so he pulled out the skis until they were about two and a half feet long, a compromise between skates and skis.

"Good-bye, darling."

And he was gone, skate-skiing across the icy wasteland.

Guided by Penelope, he headed straight for the complex. It was almost pleasant skimming along in the pale Antarctic sun, and he would have enjoyed himself if it hadn't been for the terrible uncertainties that lay ahead in the installation. Could he alone possibly cripple this enormous and well-organized scheme that might very well destroy the world? Or was he being a quixotic idiot?

"Behind you!" Penelope was suddenly warning. Sterling looked back, and there indeed was a

Hovercraft, two hundred yards back, skidding along fast, three feet above the ice on its cushion of air. Sterling began to skate as fast as he could, which was very fast indeed in spite of the moguls and depressions in the ice surface. But he was no match for the Hovercraft, which came faster, gaining on him easily.

When the Hovercraft was a hundred feet from him, Sterling turned, and skating backward, he pulled the strange-looking weapon with its big flared barrel from his waist. Holding it with both hands, he fired once at the Hovercraft. What came out of the barrel with flame and a hiss was not a bullet but a miniature missile. It sped straight for the Hovercraft, struck it in the nose, and exploded. The craft plummeted to the ice, skidded and spun across the surface like a curling iron, and then burst into flames.

Sterling skated fast away and found refuge in an icy cove behind some great blocks of ice. From there he watched the surviving soldiers, three of them, scramble out of the craft. One of them had his clothing afire, and his companion threw him down on the ice to extinguish the flames.

In a little while the three spread out in different directions, their guns at the ready, in search of their assailant. Eventually one of them saw the cove where Sterling had taken refuge, and cautiously he headed for it. From his knapsack Sterling took a collapsible device that looked like a ruler. He snapped it open and angled it into a boomerang shape. When the searcher was twenty feet from his hiding place, Sterling pressed a tiny button on the device. It hissed and then shot into the air. Unerringly it spun straight to the uniformed man, struck him on the head, and a moment before the victim sagged down unconscious, it hissed obediently back to Sterling's hands.

Sterling ran to the man and dragged his limp form back into the cove. The other two searchers were almost invisible in the white distance. He took his pulse, then placed two antifreezing adhesive bandages on each side of his chest. At the same time he saw another Hovercraft arriving and settling next to the craft that he had crippled. Soldiers were getting out of it.

"You'll be all right in half an hour or so," Sterling said as he donned the unconscious man's uniform. "I hope to be able to say the same of myself."

CHAPTER FIFTEEN

Sterling joined the other men in the search for himself. Finally the Hovercraft sounded a siren to indicate that the search was over and to return to the craft.

Once inside the cabin and on the way to the installation, Sterling looked around at the dozen or so uniformed men. No one talked. They seemed men of extraordinary discipline . . . and of all types and nationalities. A few Americans, but some clearly English, Russian, German, and Scandinavian.

"Mercenaries," thought Sterling. Of course. Perfect for an operation like this. By using men privately recruited, the Americans and Soviets were managing to maintain that much sought balance of loyalty and efficiency. Just like the Englishman

who had tried to kill him . . . that private entre-
preneur of death . . . how useful he must have
been to the operation. Each killing was just a job
to him; guided by no loyalty, he didn't care whom
he was requested to snuff out. True soldiers and
dedicated officers can leak information . . .
higher pay, other temptations, make tongues
loose. But not to professional people with a vested
interest—good pay and a bonus—in such a colossal
project.

As they came closer to the installation, Sterling
began to worry about his ID . . . surely with so
many men on such a sensitive project, they must
have a highly sophisticated security system.

The answer came quickly once they had docked
at platform epsilon. The first men off the Hovercraft went through an arch not unlike an airport
metal-detector check. The officer in charge
checked a TV screen and the men went through.

Sterling tried to appear casual when it was his
turn. The officer seemed to study him longer than
usual, then glanced at the TV screen which
flashed "No. 7899A, James Ericson" and pushed
him through the turnstile. Sterling was quickly
lost in the confusion. Everyone seemed to have
some assignment. There was a lot of noise, many
unfamiliar and strange sounds.

"So I'm good old Jim Ericson," he thought.
How did that work? He saw the TV camera angled down at his sleeve. He looked at it and saw a

small patch sewn on with vertical bars on it, like on packages in supermarkets for fast computer pricing. Where had he seen that before? His mind jumped back. Greystoke had worn an identical marker on his collar! The chimp was somehow connected to this project!

The gravity beam projector back in Connecticut, the unclassified laboratory, Alfreds, Greystoke, and the President were all pieces of the same puzzle.

And where was his humanoid friend, poor old Greystoke? Was he actually here? Yes, of course, he would be here as a laboratory animal, a guinea pig.

Coming around a corner in the big tunnel, he saw him: It was Greystoke in a security cage being loaded onto an electric vehicle by a winch.

"Okay, loosen those chains on the cage," a sergeant was saying. "And get this guy over to the observation area quick. They're bitchin' already that he's late."

Greystoke spotted Sterling, and in spite of the electrodes all over his head, he held on to the bars of his cage and jumped up and down hooting excitedly. As Sterling came up, one of the guards grinned and said, "Boy, have you got chimp appeal!"

"Darwin was right," said Sterling. "He knows I'm his uncle."

"Well, he sure hates my guts," said the man.

Before they drove Greystoke away, screaming pitifully, Sterling surreptitiously made the sign for "later."

Outside the complex the three welded-together helicopters went into action. The engineers attached the chains from their undercarriage to the hooks embedded in the great blocks of precut ice. At a signal the copters' engines shattered the silence with a roar, they arose, lifting the blocks that covered the laser beam tunnels.

As the crucial time came closer and the tensions and distraction of the assignments grew, Sterling had more and more freedom in his movements. When he came to a corridor off the main tunnel, he ducked in, and safely away from the angle of the surveying TV camera, he attached a magnetic device on the wall. He repeated that in two other strategic places.

Then he asked Penelope to locate the air-conditioning control. She did in a second, drawing a map of the corridors, and Sterling set off for it at a run, which was one way to go unnoticed since all the other men in the complex seemed to be running to or from someplace. As he approached the Air Conditioning Control Room, he saw an officer shouting orders to a group of men. The officer stopped Sterling, looked at his name tag, and said, "You, too, Ericson . . . follow these men to electrical! On the double!"

"Can't, sir," said Sterling. "Special orders from

Professor Alfreds . . . something wrong with the air conditioning."

The officer hesitated, then dismissed him with a wave, and Sterling stepped into the control room. It was empty. Frantically he studied the maze of switches and cables and wires.

"Help," he said to Penelope.

With her assistance he found the right wires, and with his small wire cutter he severed three of them. Then he welded them onto a terminal, a remote-control device tuned into a tiny triggering mechanism that he put into his pocket. Then he shoved everything back in place, cleaned up the cuttings, and left the room hurriedly.

"Now what, sir?" asked Penelope.

"Greystoke," he said. "Lead me to him."

"He is already installed in the observation point which is—"

At that moment a voice announced over the loudspeaker, "Clear all tunnels, clear all tunnels, all personnel clear all tunnels. Freon process begins in T minus two minutes!"

"You were saying?" prompted Sterling.

"Which is ten minutes by foot away from where you are standing."

"We don't have ten minutes . . . we seem to have only two!"

His eyes caught a guard who sped up on a streamlined electric motor bike, parked it hurriedly, and ran down a corridor. Sterling quickly jumped on the vehicle and in a moment was speeding down the main corridor, against the tide of men all running in the opposite direction. Some looked at him curiously and one yelled, "Where the hell are you going, soldier?"

The voice on the public-address system was already blaring, "Freon process begins in T minus one minute. All personnel clear all tunnels . . ."

Then Penelope's directions led him to a circular area off the main corridor. In the center on a raised dais, Greystoke, moaning pitifully, was strapped and chained to a cement bench, dressed in his astronaut suit with oxygen mask and electrodes coming out of his helmet like the snakes out of Medusa's head. He chattered and screamed with excitement when he saw Sterling, who immediately undid the straps on the chimp's arms and legs.

"T minus forty seconds, Sterling," warned Penelope.

Sterling took out his laser pen, cut through the metal straps, and Greystoke threw his arms around his savior. They ran for the electric bike, and Sterling headed straight for the vertical laser beam tunnels.

Professor Alfreds looked up from his controls and vital monitors and happened to see, on one of the twenty less important monitors, the image of a man and an ape on an electric vehicle.

"I don't believe it!" he exclaimed. Then in a whisper to himself: "It is Sterling Mann! That bungling idiot! Why is he interfering with my experiment? What is he doing with that ape? He is mad!"

Then, tersely, he gave the order to proceed with the freon process.

"Regrettably, we lose the chimpanzee and his reactions," he said coldly. "It is a major loss! We also lose Mr. Mann. That is a minor loss. Proceed!"

Sterling was a quarter of a mile from the first tunnel exit when the electric vehicle jerked twice and glided to a stop, its electrical power totally depleted.

He tried vainly to start it again, then he grabbed the chimp in his arms and raced frantically down the tunnel.

"Tunnels A, B, and C . . . seal!" came the command over the loudspeaker in a doomsday voice.

Sterling could hear the doors being electronically slammed shut. A confirming voice on the speakers announced: "Tunnels A, B, and C now in vacuum."

Sterling and Greystoke almost made it to the last door but it closed in their faces. Sterling took a deep breath, saw that Greystoke's mask was in place and that he was breathing normally, then commanded Penelope to open the door.

In a moment she came back with: "Sterling, all doors have been disconnected from main control computer."

Already the vacuum was getting to him; his

lungs were burning and his ears were buzzing. He had very little time.

And Alfreds, watching Sterling and the chimp, also was finding it hard to breathe . . . but because of his emotions. Watching a decent, highly intelligent man and a valuable, almost human animal expire. But it was in the name of science! It was vital! No sacrifice was too great for the ultimate good of humanity. He hesitated as the seconds were ticking away.

"It's time, Professor," said one of the assistants who was checking the computer readout.

Alfreds put his hand to his aching forehead, turned away from the monitor, and whispered the command: "Freonize!"

As the clouds of freon gas started to sweep through the tunnels, Sterling, knowing that he had less than a minute to live, took out the low-helium laser pen, adjusted to its maximum searing intensity, and like a jigsaw with plywood, he cut out a circle around the locking device. He pushed open the door and dragged Greystoke through it. After a huge breath of clean air, he then adjusted the pen to wide beam and melted the hole, sealing the door as before. As he was doing it, he felt the whole door go freezing cold when the cloud of deadly gas swept by it.

They ran and came to a major vertical tunnel with a narrow ladder up the side; next to it arrows and stenciled instructions clearly showed that it led up to the surface.

"Up!" Sterling knelt down and signed to Grey-stoke, pointing to the ladder. "Climb high . . . come to cold! Go that way." He pointed southeast. "Close by . . . find Melanie! You remember Mel-ane? She's near, waiting for you in the hole in the ice."

The chimp nodded as if he understood, and Sterling lowered the sun visor on the animal's hel-met and gave him a hug. Then Greystoke scamp-ered to the ladder and scrambled up it fast.

Sterling looked both ways, saw no one coming, and went up the same ladder. At the second floor he stepped off.

Not far away Professor Alfreds noted with pounding heart that the exact moment had almost come, that the satellite was in perfect synchroni-zation with the lab's laser reflectors. It was ren-dezvous time.

"Activate the laser beams!" he commanded in a breathy voice.

"Power generators giving maximum output," came back a voice over the intercom.

Then: "Reflectors now swung into place!"

On the monitor Alfreds saw the beginning of his dream unfold: beams, giant blood-red beams, shot up into the heavens, even the tunnels were bathed in the blinding glow of the laser light.

"Oh, God," whispered the agnostic Alfreds. "Oh, God, oh, God."

Meanwhile, Melanie, half asleep in her hole in the ice, was awakened by the light, and she watched with amazement as the two huge laser beams stabbed up into the sky from the Antarctic floor. So mesmerized by the pyrotechnics, she wasn't aware of an alien presence near her. Then she saw the hulking, menacing shadow above her at the rim of the hole. She fumbled for the pistol and managed to squeeze the trigger for one shot. At the flame and the noise she fell back against the side of the hole, and then suddenly she heard herself scream as a hairy hand caressed her face.

"Jesus!" she exclaimed as she looked into the soulful brown eyes. "Greystoke! Are you all right! Thank God I'm lousy with guns!"

The chimpanzee cooed and stroked her hair gently. She hugged him tightly as somehow his presence indicated that Sterling was alive and safe.

In the laboratory the droning sound of collossal generators was heard all over, and as Sterling emerged from a side entrance into the main corridor, he could hear Alfreds's voice announcing triumphantly over the loudspeakers: "The lasers have interlocked in space! Let the proton accelera- tion commence . . . all systems are go!"

It was easy for Sterling to find the control room—it was on sort of an island connected to the main corridor by a narrow bridge. Sterling started running . . . and found himself facing an armed guard at the end of the bridge. He ducked down below the man's rifle, reached up and struck him a karate blow to the kidney, and then lifted him up and over the bridge to fall to the floor below. This was observed by a security officer on a monitor who triggered the general alarm. Guards began sweeping the area around the control room looking for the intruder.

"Enemy presence closing in fast," Penelope warned.

"Activate Units H!" Sterling commanded.

There was a loud buzzing sound, and at the same time three armed guards appeared from a passageway leading to the main corridor. They saw three men dressed like Sterling Mann, all looking like Sterling Mann, each with a pistol aimed toward them. At the same moment five more guards appeared at the entrance across the corridor. They had automatic weapons at the ready, and when they saw the three Sterling Manns, they began to fire. The bullets went through the holographic images and some of the lead struck the opposite wall and ricocheted, but two bullets hit their own firing soldiers across the way and felled them. Another burst by both sides and another soldier fell wounded.

Meanwhile, the fourth—and real—Sterling Mann had taken advantage of the confusion to head for the control room. He opened the door and burst into the large anteroom, only fifty feet from the central control room and Alfreds. In front of him stood two armed guards.

"Hello," he said as casually as he could and shrugged. He glanced at the large air-conditioning vents. The two men were each near a vent. Little ribbons tied to the grates fluttered out actively.

"Got to speak to Doctor Alfreds . . . emergency . . . big alert!"

"He's alerted," growled the sergeant, raising his rifle. "And you are the emergency."

"Come now," Sterling said ingratiatingly. "I'm not that much of a threat. Let me speak to Professor Alfreds for a moment."

Sterling had his hand in his pocket, and he pressed the remote-control device's button. Instantly the ribbons that had been blowing out suddenly were sucked in by the great reversal of air. The same powerful suction yanked the rifles from the hands of the men and as Sterling flung himself to the floor underneath the currents, the two men were jerked off their feet and slammed up against the vents. They hung there, stuck to the wall, mouths open in terror and surprise, arms and legs working ridiculously, like two impaled butterflies.

Sterling rolled away on the floor from the air currents and then stood up . . . to find himself face to face with two guards in front of the door to the control room. They raised their automatic guns at the same time that a voice blared over the speakers: "Attention all security personnel, holographic images of the intruder are being projected in certain areas, namely F, G, and K. Do not, repeat, do *not* shoot at the intruder. They are only images and you may injure yourselves or others."

At this announcement the two soldiers looked at

Sterling uncertainly and then at each other and lowered their rifles. Their brief lapse of attention gave Sterling the chance to double one up with a crushing kick to the shins and then catch the other with a slashing backhand chop to the side of the jaw, which felled him where he stood.

"Congratulations," said Penelope. "Though I regret your resorting to brute force."

"Shut up and do two things for me and do them fast, sweetheart," Sterling whispered. "First, activate Melanie's getaway gismo. Second, figure how to get me into that locked control room around the corner."

"There is a guard there."

"Okay, I'll take care of him," Sterling said. "What about the lock?"

"I must have greater proximity to it."

"Greater proximity you shall have, sweetheart."

Outside Melanie was dozing off in her make-shift igloo when Greystoke's prodding awakened her with a start. The chimp kept pointing to the large package and the light on top which was blinking red.

"My God!" whispered Melanie, confused. "What did he say . . . something about yellow? Red meant get ready . . . but for what?"

What weird thing had Sterling Mann dreamed up now? Greystoke chattered excitedly as the light went to green and the compact package began to swell before their eyes.

In the underground lab Sterling peered cautiously around the corner at the control room. Penelope was right, only one guard. He took the low-helium pen from his pocket, took the cap off it, and put it on the back. It contained condensed missile fuel, and he aimed it at the guard. The man saw him, saw some kind of weapon aimed at him, and quickly raised his rifle. But he was too late, for Sterling had pressed the clip and the pen fired with a loud hiss. The guard clutched his chest and pitched forward.

Sterling ran to the heavy metal door and held Penelope to the lock.

"Don't screw up, madam!" urged Sterling.

"It is a time lock," said Penelope. "But, no problem. I have that specialized information."

In a few seconds the mechanism clicked open and Sterling burst into the room. Alfreds swiveled away from the controls in his chair, and he had a little wry, but triumphant, smile on his face.

"Professor Alfreds . . ." Sterling started to say, but then something hard hit him on the back of his head and he fell to his knees and then sprawled on the floor.

He came to shortly thereafter in a dizzy cloud, looking into the black barrel of a pistol held by one uniformed man. Except for his assailant, Dr. Alfreds at the controls, and a woman assistant, there was no one else in the room.

"I suggest you behave yourself, Mr. Mann," said Alfreds coolly. "In a few minutes everything will be over, and we will put you on a plane back

to Washington. Although you have tried everything in your power to harm this experiment."

"Alfreds," said Sterling, hoarsely, "you are on a
collision course."

"I am?" Alfreds smiled contentedly. "But this is
the meaning of the experiment. A collision."

"No, you don't understand. The experiment is
wrong and you are going to destroy the world,
maybe the universe!"

Alfreds smiled enigmatically and said, "Pity."

Sterling continued, "You are a great scientist;
you are also a good person, but you have overlooked one important factor along the line."

Alfreds swiveled his chair back to his monitors.
"And what is the factor I've overlooked?" he
asked.

"The mirror factor."

He swiveled his chair back to face Sterling. His
face was serious. "The mirror factor?"

"The experiment seems to be leading to the beginning of the world but it is not. It is as if you are
looking at whatever you expect in a mirror. It is
the opposite. It is leading you to the end of the
world instead."

Alfreds sighed. "Medieval philosophy, Mann.
Dangerous philosophy and superstition." He
turned to a girl in a white robe. "All right, my
dear," he said, "prepare for computer interlock."

She nodded and pressed a few touch-switches
with the expertise of a good typist.

Sterling realized the experiment was well on its

way. Whatever alternatives he had, he should play without risking Melanie's life. He touched the heat-sensitive command of his wrist terminal, and in three short bursts and one long one, he activated the final stage of Melanie's transportation out of hell.

The guard watched Sterling's hand movements curiously.

"Hey . . . that's some fancy watch!" he said suspiciously. He reached down and pulled the watch off Sterling's wrist and strapped it on his own.

"Suits you fine," said Sterling, knowing that Penelope would already be analyzing tissue type, blood pressure, and temperature, aware now that a stranger was wearing the instrument. "Yes, I think you and that thing were made for each other," said Sterling.

In fifteen seconds the watch emitted a twenty-thousand-volt impulse, the uniformed man stiffened, his eyes rolled in his head, and he pitched forward to the floor. Sterling grabbed the pistol from his hand, and leaping forward, he held the weapon to Alfreds's head.

He ordered the assistant into a small room in the rear and locked the door.

"Now, sir, we negotiate!"

In her shelter Melanie's eyes grew wider and Greystoke hugged her with fear as the green package blossomed into a larger and larger balloon as it filled with helium. And then Melanie saw the "yellow area" that Sterling had emphasized: It started as a square, then became a yellow gondola that unfolded like the collapsible metal cups that come in picnic baskets.

She took Greystoke by the hand, and quickly they climbed into the basket as the great balloon filled. Then slowly it rose from the icy waste, silently, gracefully, eerily.

Greystoke looked at her questioningly but trustingly.

"You want to know where we're going, don't you, Greystoke?" said Melanie with an attempt to smile reassurance to the animal. "Well, so do I. But I imagine that this"—she patted the metal box in the gondola that housed the radio compass—"is set to carry us to the nearest civilized area. I can hardly wait to see brown land and kangaroos and take a hot bath!"

"What do you know about Vasilief?" Sterling asked, the gun in his hand pointing at Alfreds's chest.

"Stop this stupid interrogation, Mann. A discussion about Vasilief will not slow down the protons. They are already in their programmed course. Nothing can stop them."

"What do you know about Vasilief?" Sterling repeated.

"A great scientist of his time. Who knows, if he had not been working in the Soviet Union, he might have discovered the atom bomb."

"He did."

Alfreds took his eyes off the board. "What's this nonsense? Vasilief died long before atomic energy."

"Vasilief is not dead. He is still alive, and he knew about atomic energy, matter and antimatter long before you were born, Professor."

Alfreds took the news with, "You are not telling me the truth. You are bluffing."

"Not at a moment like this. Vasilief was responsible for the Tungusky incident."

"Tungusky! Vasilief? Oh, my God!"

All of a sudden the scientist in Alfreds was taking over, and he started to consider the validity of Sterling's words.

Sterling continued. "Vasilief says you are going to blast the universe to pieces. He says this experiment will backfire."

"But why?" Alfreds murmured to himself. "How? This is something I studied for twenty years . . ."

"It is the magnitude of the experiment, sir, not the principle." Sterling pointed. "Now please stop the acceleration."

"Even if I wanted to—and I don't—I could not abort this experiment. After phase one, the computer took over, developed an interlock system to prevent sabotage of the very type you've been attempting. Even if the laser beams are shut down, the protons will still make their journey into the

tunnels and they will collide as programmed
. . . although not the way I had hoped."

He then pointed toward a special monitor that
showed what he meant in a microphotographic
process. Penelope confirmed its veracity: "The
proton collision can't be stopped," she said.

In frustration Sterling banged the barrel of the
pistol into the palm of his hand. "There's got to be
a way," he mused.

"Not if I don't know it," said Penelope.

And then it came to him.

"You are a splendid creation," murmured Sterling. "But unfortunately, or fortunately, you don't
know everything. There's still a place for human
logic."

Short circuit was the answer! Short out the
power lines to the laser beams! But how?

He asked Penelope to find the wires in the
great control box which governed the servo-
mechanism of the reflectors of the beams. She indicated the big red and blue wires, and Sterling
put down the pistol and pulled out a pair of wire
clippers from his jacket. Before Penelope could
warn him that the wires themselves were "hot," a
defense mechanism powered to prevent tamper-
ing, Sterling held the two wires together and cut
them both. As he did, hundreds of volts slammed
through his body.

"Fool!" exclaimed Alfreds. He made no move to
pull the paralyzed man from the wires that held

him by the clippers in his hand. Alfreds knew that if he touched Sterling, the same voltage would be transferred to his body also.

Sterling, unable to let go, felt his eyes bulging from his head, could smell his own flesh burning, could feel himself losing consciousness. And then a vein on the back of his right hand burst, and the spurting blood spilled onto the severed ends of the wires.

All the controls in the room were short-circuited. The lights on the control board and the TV monitors went off, and Sterling sagged back against the wall, breathing hard, clutching his hand, and close to fainting. But he saw Alfreds glance at the pistol, and he shook his head to clear it and lurched forward and grabbed the weapon.

"Congratulations, Sterling," said Penelope. "Sometimes the human mind is better than a computer's . . . but not often. You have succeeded in causing the laser beams to weaken and fade. The acceleration of the protons cannot now be as powerful."

"But it will still take place?" Sterling gasped.

"Yes, the backup systems are now reprogramming the acceleration. The internal collision though will not be as big as originally planned."

"Can't you stop it altogether . . . jam something?"

"Negative. I suggest you get out of there as soon as possible."

"Good suggestion. Can you also suggest how?"

"Submarines."

"Submarines?"

"There is an underwater launching area for miniature submarines not far away."

"Guide me," Sterling said. Then to Alfreds, "Get up . . . we're getting out of here."

Alfreds shook his head. "I'm not. You go ahead. Make your way out if you can. But I'm staying. The experiment isn't ruined yet. The answer will be more vague, more difficult to understand, but I must see it through."

"You have two hundred and forty seconds," Penelope cut in. "You must move quickly."

"Sorry, Professor. I can't leave you here," said Sterling, pushing his pistol into Alfreds's back. "Your life is too precious to waste on a failure like this."

Alfreds tried to resist, but Sterling had opened the electronically controlled sliding door and pushed the older man ahead of him.

"Two hundred and five seconds," Penelope warned.

They walked toward a tunnel. Many guards were running to it from several directions and Sterling was prepared for an encounter, but none of the guards paid any attention to them. A voice over the loudspeakers was instructing "all personnel in red alert, report immediately to security zone omega."

"Why is the computer instructing an abort if there is no danger?" Sterling asked.

"The computer is programmed to safeguard the people in case of malfunction. You cut down the lasers. The computer reads that as malfunction."

Suddenly Alfreds stopped. "Please, let me stay . . ."

Without replying, Sterling took him by the arm and they started running.

"One hundred and eighty-five seconds," Penelope informed Sterling.

They arrived at the hydraulic lift as Penelope was counting one hundred seconds exactly.

The two-man elevator descended quietly sixty feet down into the ice. A blast of cold air hit them in the face as the elevator door slid shut behind them. The lone guard didn't make it to his automatic weapon before Sterling hit him. There were three small submarines, not much larger than oversized torpedoes, lying in the water, hatches open.

"If the experiment was foolproof, why the getaway devices?" asked Sterling as he pushed Alfreds firmly into one of the submarines.

"All foolproof projects have a way out . . . for cowards or fools," he replied. "Please, for the last time, let me stay with my project," Alfreds pleaded.

"I know it was your life, Peofessor, but it needn't be your death," Sterling reasoned as he checked over the controls, which he found fairly simple to operate.

The hatch closed electronically and the submarine sank slowly into the pitch-black waters under the ice.

"Forty-five seconds," said Penelope.

In the safety of zone omega the personnel of the giant lab watched quietly as the screen faded to black; they watched riveted as the cameras inside the tunnel that housed the rendezvous sensors came to life. The digital countdown in hot red flashing numerical figures continued.

All lights inside the tunnel were switched off by the main computer; the lights inside zone omega were dimmed.

"Collision minus ten seconds," the digital informer read.

They stared, holding their breath, as the protons racing close to the speed of light were automatically diverted to an opposite course and, as the countdown continued on to zero, switched into a common tunnel.

There was no sound. Nothing. A few seconds ticked away, and the worried scientists exchanged questioning glances.

Then, out of the darkness, the camera recorded a faint glow. The computer verified success. Smiles spread to many faces and people started to move. And then it hit them. The dim phosphorescent glow of the resulting collision multiplied with stunning velocity. The green glow became amber and strong in intensity. The computer bombarded the screen with endless digits. A sound, like the echo from a collapsing catacomb, wailed through the speakers and became audible even through the thick steel walls; a tremor shook the solid, massive floor and the lights flickered in an alarming manner.

The amber glow became blinding white. Now the tremor was shaking zone omega even though it was a safety area, hydraulically suspended to absorb all vibrations. The camera inside the tunnel melted in a fraction of a second. The computer issued a frantic warning, EXPERIMENT IN CRITICAL STAGE, which flashed for an instant, then faded from the screen. Tiny blue bulbs came to life through an auxiliary power system. The two hundred and seventy people in zone omega moved to the sealed exits as the tremor became unbearable. Some lay on the floor, their eyes bulging, while others grabbed desperately at the walls. Cries filled the air.

In the final collision tunnel the microblast was multiplying with the speed of light. Tragically confirming Sterling's worry, the protons, so safe when they collided under normal acceleration, now had gained uncontrollable speed "riding" the laser beams and had started a chain reaction. The cosmic "glue" in Vasilief's theory became the ultimate catalyst, and the particles, which under other circumstances would be unnoticed by the naked eye, gained in substance and energy. The more the microblast multiplied, the higher the speed of the colliding protons became. It was like a giant cosmic amoeba, spreading through the

sealed tunnel, vaporizing everything in sight.
Metal melted in a fraction of a second and turned
into hot steam. The heat generated by the resulting nuclear blast blew the magnets storing antimatter so that it was released uncontrolled
throughout the tunnels and the storage areas. As
soon as the ten-inch steel door of the main tunnel
turned into hot vapor, the computer lost control
over the complex and all safety doors slid open.

The loudspeakers continued spitting out prere-
corded instructions that no one could hear. People
were running in panic when the freon system exploded, sweeping sixty people to an instant frosty
death; then the nuclear wave followed, charring
the frozen bodies and smothering the tunnels.

The recorded instructions died on the speakers
that now filled the air with a deafening static.

It took seventy-five seconds for the raging nuclear fire to reach the core of the installation—the
gigantic plutonium reactor that had automatically
shut itself off. The serpent of blinding light engulfed the cylindrical reactor and dipped quickly
to its guts, setting off the ultimate nuclear blast.

Far above the Antarctic ice cap, Melanie's balloon glided silently, as if she were in some opiate,
purposeless dream. Yet from time to time the still-
ness would be shattered by the brief roar of the
small jet tubes on each side of the basket that
were triggered by the automatic radio pilot, programmed to guide the balloon to Tasmania.

But Melanie was not thinking of her own or

even Greystoke's safety. Her eyes were transfixed by the faint glow under the ice. She was horrified as she saw it go from purple to orange to yellow and finally to bright white. And she saw the ice turn to vapor for a radius of almost a hundred miles.

And she sobbed uncontrollably as she turned her head away from the terrible scene. Greystoke didn't understand, but he stroked her hair gently and made the sign for "hungry."

CHAPTER SIXTEEN

The flight from Sydney was exhausting, and the little sleep Melanie could get was filled with nightmares. The balloon had taken her on a flawless course to Tasmania and from there she was driven to the nearest airport. The authorities in Australia were alerted and they asked no questions. Nicholas Meyers, ever the faithful butler, was at the airport to pick up Melanie and Greystoke when they returned to New York. Nicholas's serious face revealed no emotion, but his eyes, Melanie thought, were moist. He bowed stiffly to Melanie in his characteristic fashion. Uncharacteristically, however, he shed his reserve and picked up Greystoke and hugged him, as though it were all right to show emotion with animals but not with humans. He never would have hugged the animal's late master, but it was permissible to hug the man's pet . . . in absentia . . . in memoriam.

An hour later the Rolls was parked in the building's garage and they entered the penthouse. It seemed bleak, cold, and silent . . . even Penelope was switched off. Nicholas, like a new grandfather, promptly took Greystoke off to the kitchen to feed him delicacies. Melanie went on to the guest room like an automaton.

Suddenly, alone for the first time in days, she was unable to hold back the tears any longer and, throwing herself across the bed, was engulfed in quiet expression of her grief. Her face was hidden between her outflung arms, and only the shaking of her shoulders and an occasional stertorous intake of breath indicated how profoundly she had been overcome.

Finally, much relieved, she sat up and after a moment went to bathe her face and swollen eyes. The intercom buzzer sounded and she answered it.

"Shall-you-be-coming-out-to-dinner-or-shall-you-wish-a-tray-miss?" came the automated voice of Nicholas.

Knowing his grief to be as deep as her own for the beloved Sterling, she felt obliged to make the effort and replied, "I'm not really hungry, but I'll come out shortly, Nicholas. I think a glass of sherry would be nice."

"Thank-you-miss-I-understand-miss."

As Melanie came into the spacious living room, her glass of sherry was waiting on the cocktail table. She was about to pick it up when she saw the note. Was it Sterling's handwriting? Her heart jumped. "Look to the west," was all it said. To the west was the huge picture window. Melanie walked to the window . . . slowly, in wonder.

It was dusk now and New York City was glowing at her feet, and lonely . . . in a way as vast and lonely as Antarctica.

What did it mean . . . look at what to the west? There was Times Square. The huge illuminated cartoon board, the famous clichéd symbol of Broadway, glittered and flickered, dominating the scene. As she watched the animated sign, she realized that two gigantic hands were forming words in sign language . . .

"I AM ALIVE . . . I AM WELL . . ."

Melanie stared in disbelief, wanting to believe but afraid to believe, then the animated hands again formed: "I AM ALIVE . . . I AM WELL . . ."

Melanie's eyes welled with tears of joy as she began to believe the message was really from Sterling.

Then: "I LOVE YOU . . . I LOVE YOU . . ."

She watched in fascination as the hands then made the signs for "LOOK BEHIND YOU . . ."

Melanie whirled around. And there he was! Sterling was actually there! Or was he? She said, "You are not real . . . you are . . . holography!"

But she knew it was not a holographic image when Sterling took her into his arms and kissed her . . . he was real . . . very real.

CHAPTER SEVENTEEN

It was a very gloomy afternoon in Washington, D.C. The President paced his office, looking at the two visitors. Professor Alfreds studied the carpet on the floor; Sterling was looking out the window at the raindrops piling up on the glass and then coursing down it. The two had escaped the explosion in the fast miniature submarine and had made it to the coast of Australia. A U.S. Air Force plane had taken them back to Washington.

The President stopped pacing and sat in his chair.

"They've informed me that the nuclear blast has raised fear and worry around the world," he said. "We have agreed to blame it on the Russians and the Russians, naturally, will blame it on us. For the next twenty months we will be getting very confusing weather reports. And fallout . . . what about fallout?"

Alfreds shook his head. "None," he said. "All safely under the ice."

The President broke a pencil with his fingers. "What the hell went wrong?" he asked in a calm but raging voice.

Alfreds continued to look at the floor as he replied, "Perhaps . . . perhaps, Mr. President, we are not yet ready for such a big jump ahead. Perhaps nature, after all, is entitled to keep some of her secrets from science."

The President rolled his eyes to the ceiling. "I didn't ask for pathetic excuses about our defeat. I want to know what the hell happened there!"

Sterling spoke up. "Let's say, Mr. President, that it was human error. We will never find out. Perhaps the companies that manufactured the components used inadequate materials. Perhaps it was computer miscalculation. The fact is that with Professor Alfreds's quick and efficient reaction to the resulting problem, the world was saved."

"And we lost face to the Russians, who had wanted to control the experiment in the first place. They will never forgive the billions they spent on such a stupid, doomed project. How can we expect their cooperation again?"

"The Russians will go back to the drawing board," said Sterling.

Alfreds looked at the President, eyes shining

with anticipation as he asked, "What about us, Mr. President?"

The President looked at Sterling. "What *about* us, Mr. Mann? You seemed to know right from the beginning what was happening. What about us?"

Sterling gave him a reassuring smile. "We'll survive, sir. We'll go back to the drawing board, too."

"Goddamn right," said the President as he lit a cigar. "We are a great country," he said as he blew out a puff of smoke. "We'll manage to surface winners." He looked at his watch. "Thank you, gentlemen," he said. "Time to call it a day." Looking out the window, he mumbled, "Nice weather," sarcastically to himself.

Professor Alfreds uttered a sad good night as he turned to the door.

Sterling was about to follow Alfreds when the President raised his finger, indicating that he wanted Sterling to stay. When the door closed behind Alfreds, the President put his cigar in an ashtray and looked at Sterling conspiratorially. "One thing I want to know," he said. "Is Alfreds to be trusted? Does he really know what he's doing, or is he a senile old man, playing God with my support and the taxpayers' money?"

Sterling looked pensive but remained silent.

"Well?"

"I might be better able to answer your question if you'd be kind enough to answer some of mine."

The President gave a consenting nod.

"I never saw any Russians in this whole operation. Were there really any Russians involved?"

The President smiled. "Not many of them," he said. He drew closer to Sterling and winked. "The deal was simple. We would put up some money and the know-how, and they would put up more money—and the silence. They didn't trust the CIA or any other agency, and we didn't trust the KGB either. So the decision was to hire mercenaries, private contractors, private operatives."

Sterling considered for a moment, then asked, "But why Alexandra? Why me?"

The President looked him directly in the eye and said, "The deal with the Russians was that whether it be one of us or one of them that might jeopardize the security of the project, the private operatives were to make no exception."

"Thank you, Mr. President," said Sterling. "Now, to answer your question. No, Professor Alfreds is not senile. He really is a great scientist but he may simply have been trapped in his own truth."

The President smiled and nodded as he looked out of the window.

"And, Mr. President, please don't get any more ideas."

The President shook his head. "Thank you, Mr. Mann. I'm glad we have you on the payroll."

Dr. Monroe was waiting in the limousine for Sterling when he saw Professor Alfreds come out of the White House, his head almost buried in his chest. Instinctively Monroe wanted to call to him, to shake his hand and offer a few encouraging words, but he didn't move from his seat behind the tinted glass. He was afraid that his presence close to Sterling one more time might trigger suspicions. He watched silently as the old man stopped, then stood looking up at the sky as if suddenly aware of the rain.

Sterling came out and, bounding down the stairs, saw Alfreds and veered toward him. Coming up behind the older man, he took him by the arm and gently escorted him to another limousine.

As the old scientist got into the car, he said, "One thing, Mr. Mann . . . someone must have tutored you. Not only your knowledge of science, but the fantastic awareness, all that makes you so different. Your father, perhaps?"

Sterling glanced back at Dr. Monroe's blurred profile behind the dripping glass and said, quietly, "My father . . . perhaps."

Alfreds gave him a look of genuine affection as he said, "Lucky man."

The limousine drove off.